I0720011

A

GRAVE

SECRET

STAR OF JUSTICE SERIES

A
GRAVE
SECRET

STAR OF JUSTICE SERIES

BRUCE HAMMACK

BOOKS BY BRUCE HAMMACK

THE SMILEY AND MCBLYTHE MYSTERY SERIES
Exercise Is Murder, Prequel
Jingle Bells, Rifle Shells
Pistols and Poinsettias
Five Card Murder
Murder In The Dunes
The Name Game Murder
Murder Down The Line
Vision Of Murder
Mistletoe, Malice And Murder
A Beach To Die For
Dig Deep For Murder

THE FEN MAGUIRE MYSTERY SERIES
Murder On The Brazos
Murder On The Angelina
Murder On The Guadalupe
Murder On The Wichita
Murder On The San Gabriel

STAR OF JUSTICE SERIES
The Long Road to Justice
A Murder Redeemed
A Grave Secret
Justice On A Midnight Clear

See a current catalog of books at brucehammack.com/books

CHAPTER ONE

Sleep had almost overtaken CJ when the door to her bedroom flew open. She squinted against the glare of the overhead light. "What's wrong?"

"Get dressed," said David.

She didn't bother asking why until she was halfway to the closet, pulling off a T-shirt as she went.

Her husband spoke loud enough for her to hear from inside the walk-in closet. "I've been monitoring radio traffic in my office. A student is being transported to Riverview Regional. They're performing CPR."

"Any other details?"

"Not much. The call from your dispatcher said a student in Sycamore dorm was unresponsive."

Her cell phone vibrated on the nightstand. "Get that for me."

A one-sided conversation followed. "She's getting dressed... Good... No. She'll take care of it."

By the time David disconnected the call, CJ had thrown on jeans and a blouse. She carried a dark blazer in one hand and black boots in the other. Sitting on the side of the bed she opened her mouth to speak, but David beat her to it. "Lieutenant Griggs is on the scene and Maria's on her way. I told your dispatcher you'll call Alice."

"University presidents don't like to get news like this secondhand. I'll do it on the way." She looked around. "Grab my gun."

David took long strides toward a tall dresser and retrieved her .40 caliber Glock from a locked drawer. He slid in a clip and shoved the weapon into her shoulder holster. "I'll drive while you make calls."

The first phone call went to Lieutenant Griggs, the night supervisor. He'd been around long enough to know what CJ needed to hear and what she didn't. "Looks like a dorm party with high-octane booze. The girl and three others were playing some sort of drinking game."

"Was she unconscious when the first officer arrived?"

"Out cold and blue. Stephens started CPR right away and kept at it until paramedics took over."

CJ hated to ask the next question. "Any chance she'll make it?"

"They shocked her once before they loaded her. It didn't look good."

"What's her name?"

"Holly Grimes. A freshman." He paused. "I have the other three girls separated for Maria. They're all pretty wasted. Two of them filled their trash cans."

"Text me with Holly's emergency contact information. I'll need to call after I find out if she's going to make it."

"Every parent's worst nightmare," said the lieutenant.

DAVID'S STATE-ISSUED SUV streaked by the president's mansion of Agape Christian University as CJ placed the next call to Alice Cummings, the university president. The call brought the expected response of controlled grief. She thanked CJ and said she'd come to the hospital as soon as she could. CJ knew Alice would be offering up a prayer even as she dressed.

With headlamps and emergency lights punching white, red, and blue holes in the darkness, they made it through the heart of Riverview, crossed over the interstate, and arrived at the regional hospital. The emergency room doors retracted when David slid to a stop under the portico, giving CJ a clear view of the waiting room. Charlotte, a recently hired patrol officer, stood inside, looking like she didn't know what to do with her hands.

Long strides carried CJ through the doorway. "Is she going to make it?"

The blond, twenty-three-year-old lifted her shoulders and let them fall. "The doctor told me I couldn't come in. I can't get any information out of anyone."

"Come with me."

CJ dug into her pocket and pulled out her badge case. She approached the woman sitting behind a Plexiglas barrier and pushed her badge and identification against the plastic. "I'm CJ Harper, the assistant chief of police at Agape Christian University. I need to see the student that was brought in a little while ago and the attending physician."

The woman balked, but not long enough to form words. CJ added in a firm, calm voice, "This isn't a request. Open the door."

A buzzer sounded. CJ moved toward the doorway, then stopped. "Stay here, Charlotte. I'll be back when I know what's going on."

David caught up to her and they passed into a warren of hallways and treatment rooms. She spoke to the first scrubs-clad person she saw. "What room is Holly Grimes in?"

The woman looked at the small circular badge attached to David's chest and then the pistol riding on his hip. "Room five. I'll tell Dr. Ray you're here."

They cracked the door open, but no sounds came from within. CJ extended her hand and pushed as David's hand rested on her shoulder. Packaging from medical supplies littered the floor, while a bank of machines sat as silent and motionless as the body partially covered with a sheet. CJ moved toward the lifeless student with slow steps. She was a pretty girl with thick hair the color of ripe wheat and a hummingbird tattoo on the inside of her right wrist.

Footsteps coming through the door alerted husband and wife of a person's arrival. She had a round face and eyeglasses with frames that looked two sizes too big. The monogramed white lab coat identified her as a medical doctor. "Are both of you cops?"

David took care of passing out names and titles.

The woman didn't look impressed and directed her questions to CJ. "What's going on at the university? She's the second student I've treated tonight. Both showed signs of opioid overdose and alcohol abuse."

The news didn't come as much of a surprise to CJ. "We're not immune from students experimenting, especially with spring break right around the corner. Most of the time it's alcohol, but we know it's common for them to try other things. Do you know the exact cause of death?"

The doctor shoved her hands into the pockets of her lab coat. "I'm holding off until I get the results of a full tox screen. If you want an educated guess, I'd say she died from a combination of too much alcohol and fentanyl. Decreased breathing, low blood pressure, coma, and death are the classic stages of fentanyl overdose."

She stepped to Holly Grimes' lifeless body and stroked a

lock of hair away from her face. "If it's fentanyl, she won't be the last."

"Three other students were partying with her tonight," said CJ.

The doctor didn't give her a chance to finish her thoughts. "Get them here as fast as you can."

ALL IT TOOK WAS a crooked finger signaling the officer to follow. Charlotte nodded and fell in line behind David and CJ as they walked toward a quiet corner of the waiting room. CJ pulled out her cell phone and punched in the name of Lieutenant Griggs. He didn't waste time with formalities. "Did she make it?"

"No." The single word seemed insufficient, but she didn't have time to give details, even if she had any. "I need you to get those other three girls to Regional ASAP. The ER doc suspects fentanyl. Tell Maria to come here after she processes the crime scene. We're treating this as a possible homicide."

"I'll bring the three girls myself."

"No. Put them in an ambulance. They carry Narcan."

"Will do. What else do you need done?"

"That's all. I'll keep Charlotte with me. Between the three of us, we can monitor them." CJ hesitated. "Make sure they understand declining to come isn't an option."

"Will do." The call ended.

CJ turned to see Charlotte look at her with cloudy eyes. "Your first death?"

The officer gave a nod of her head. "First death. First possible homicide." She looked at David and then back at CJ. "I'm lost. I couldn't get past that woman at the admitting desk."

With a hand on her officer's shoulder CJ said, "Go back in

and tell them you need to bag all the clothes and personal effects Holly came in with. Get a nurse to help you. Wear gloves and use a new plastic trash bag."

The officer swallowed, and her gaze seemed to search for a way out of the assignment.

"You knew this day would come. You need to establish the chain of custody for evidence. Make a tag and write everything on it the way you were trained. When you're finished, come back to the waiting room and see me."

The rookie officer straightened her posture, walked with head up toward the door separating the waiting area from the treatment rooms, and motioned for the gatekeeper to open it. That's all it took.

David sidled up beside CJ and waited until the door closed behind the officer. "She'll always remember this first one."

"Yeah. If she doesn't quit, there'll be more."

An alert for an incoming text beeped. She checked her phone and sighed. "Holly's emergency contact information. Her parents live in Bell County."

David pulled out his phone. "I'll make the call."

She shook her head. "Thanks, but it's my responsibility."

The call went as CJ expected. Disbelief, denial and confusion triggered a response to rush to their daughter, as if their presence would change the outcome. CJ knew anger, blame and a desire for justice would follow in the hours and days to come. As for tonight, and many nights to come, grief would have the upper hand.

David motioned CJ to the parking lot, where she finished telling the stunned father which exit to take and extended a final condolence. Coming toward them were David's father and Alice Cummings. Alice had her arm entwined in Bob's with her hand on his forearm. She asked for a status update with only raised eyebrows. A shake of CJ's head communicated the news that ACU had lost a student. Alice's free hand clutched the silver cross around her neck.

"Lieutenant Griggs is bringing in three more students that were with Holly. The ER doctor thinks fentanyl caused her death. She suspects that's what caused another student to come to the ER tonight, too. I notified Holly's parents, and they're on the way. They should be here in about an hour."

"Fentanyl!" said David's father, like the word left a nasty taste in his mouth. "I heard a lot about that junk in prison. It's supposed to be a hundred times more powerful than morphine and fifty times stronger than heroin."

David joined in. "We don't know for sure yet if it's fentanyl."

"But we're not waiting for another student to die to find out," said CJ. She caught the sound of a siren on an east wind. "That should be them."

CHAPTER TWO

The first glimmers of a new dawn pushed darkness away from their three-hundred-acre farm when David angled his SUV under the carport of their ranch-style home. CJ loved the ease and protection of their carport. They'd both seen too many garages become glorified storage sheds while vehicles baked in the Texas sun. Besides, they had a barn that provided all the room for storage they'd ever need.

CJ went straight for the swing on the back porch and wrapped herself in a shawl she kept there for early morning pilgrimages of silent meditation and prayer. She didn't need to ask if David would bring her a cup of coffee. He always did.

Light overcame darkness and life reasserted itself. Squirrels chattered as birds of various plumages sang and squawked. Deer appeared as ghosts under the trees lining the river that passed through their property. How different this was from the antiseptic cleanliness, harsh lights, and wails of grief she'd witnessed last night. An incongruent mixture of gratitude and loss filled her as she folded her hands and poured out her heart to the One who always listens.

Steaming coffee arrived after the sun cleared the horizon, and David retreated into the house to cook breakfast. That meant she still had one mug's worth of time by herself. Well, not exactly by herself.

Voices coming from the kitchen and the desire for another shot of black stimulant signaled the next installment of her day. She stood, stretched, folded the shawl, and made her way to the back door, but not before she gave thanks for the past ten years of knowing David and their one year of marriage.

She opened the door to find a child crawling toward her at flank speed. She closed the distance, scooped up the red-haired nine-month-old and planted a series of loud kisses on his neck.

"His breakfast is almost ready," said Nancy. "Do you mind feeding him? I need to get to the library and cram before my ten o'clock chemistry lab."

In the five months since Nancy and Davey moved in, they'd made themselves at home. This morning Nancy showed up with her usual tangled thatch of carrot-colored hair.

"I've got him," said CJ. "Be sure you do something about that mop."

"That's why God made baseball caps," Nancy replied with a generous smile.

The teen's sleeping attire included a men's extra large T-shirt with a country singer's likeness emblazoned on it and a pair of mismatched socks. The woefully skinny eighteen-year-old delivered a bowl of tasteless warm cereal, pureed peaches, and a bottle of formula. Her countenance changed. "Mr. David told me about the girl that died last night. That's such a shame."

"Worse than that. An avoidable tragedy." She paused. "I'm

having second thoughts about you going to South Padre Island over spring break."

Nancy tented her hands on her hips. "Here we go. I knew this would happen."

"Don't get huffy when I've been up all night. I didn't say you can't go. All I want is your word that you won't drink, or do any drugs, or put yourself where others could get you hurt or in trouble."

Nancy took a seat and rubbed her hand over her son's head. "I have too much to lose now. The girls I'm going with are all like me, on full academic scholarships. We'll swim and take long walks on the beach, but we'll limit our games to jeopardy or scrabble. We already made pinkie promises not to drink anything harder than lemonade."

CJ held out a crooked little finger. "I want in on that promise."

At the loud insistence of Davey, CJ took off her jacket and shoveled in a spoonful of tan mush tipped with peaches. "When will you be home?"

"My last class is over at one-thirty. I'll probably be the only one to show up. All anyone is talking about is spring break." Her head dipped. "I guess now we'll be talking about the girl that died last night. That's another reason for not doing something stupid."

Nancy rose and passed David on her way out of the breakfast nook. They gave each other a high-five instead of speaking. CJ looked up from her assignment of feeding Davey. "Are you going in already? Don't you need to sleep?"

"I slept. Remember? After you and Alice dealt with Holly's parents, I conked out in a waiting room chair. I'm showered and shaved and ready to go."

"How can you do that?"

"Army training. I learned to sleep sitting up with my chin

resting on my chest. It's amazing how long you can go if you grab thirty minutes every six to eight hours."

"I'll stick with our bed. Your dad will spell me from babysitting around noon."

"You're not going in today?"

"Not unless there's another emergency. John's returning this afternoon from his chiefs of police meeting. The campus started emptying yesterday, and the shift lieutenants don't need me hovering over them."

"Does John know about Holly?"

"I'll call him as soon as I finish feeding Davey."

David dished up a parting kiss and breezed out the back door. Nancy came in with her mane corralled in a ponytail sticking through the gap in the back of a baseball cap. She wore a baggy ACU sweatshirt, jeans, and cross-trainer shoes. A backpack carried everything she needed. She bent down to give Davey a kiss, looked at CJ and giggled.

"What are you laughing about?"

"Did you take off your jacket last night?"

"No. It was freezing in the hospital. Why?"

"You must have been in a hurry getting dressed."

CJ looked down and saw the cause of Nancy's mirth. She'd forgotten to put on a bra. "Thank goodness they keep hospitals cold. I wouldn't have thought twice about shucking off my jacket if it had been warm."

A warm washcloth removed all evidence of breakfast from Davey's mouth, cheeks, and even forehead. She put him on the living room floor with a plastic ark full of toy animals and watched him crawl, stop, taste one, and move to the next. She looked out the front window and sighed. Time to make a phone call.

Chief John Sylvester, her boss, sounded out of breath when he answered. She assumed the marathon runner was out pounding the pavement before he began his trip back to Riverview.

"Good morning," she said. "What mile are you on?"

"Four. I don't have time for any more. What's up?"

"We had a freshman girl OD last night."

His first response was a groan. He followed up with, "Accidental?"

"It looks like it, but we're treating it as a homicide for now. The initial tox screen was positive for opioids. The ER doc thinks it could be fentanyl. We won't know for sure until we get the forensics from the autopsy."

"Let's pray it isn't. We've been lucky so far with that stuff. Anything else?"

"Another student went to the ER last night with similar symptoms. Paramedics administered Narcan on the way. We also sent three other girls that were partying with the dead girl to the ER. No drugs, but they had plenty of alcohol to make them drunk and sick."

A few seconds of silence followed. "You notified Alice?"

"She and Bob came to the hospital. The girls' parents showed up and Alice took them to the chapel after David and I gave them what details we could."

"I don't want to think about how I'd react if it was one of our girls."

CJ didn't know if he directed the words to her or if he was thinking out loud, so she didn't respond.

"Are you going in today?" asked John.

"I'm on call. I haven't been to bed yet, and the campus is all but cleared out. Bob relieves me of my babysitting duties at noon. I'll come in this afternoon if you need me."

"Stay home. You've earned time off. Did Maria come in last night?"

"She processed the scene and interviewed witnesses."

"I'll get the details from her and follow up with Alice this afternoon." He hesitated. "Anything else?"

"One more thing. The girl that died and three others were drinking high-octane moonshine. It was clear and came in water bottles."

"Moonshine and fentanyl. That's a deadly combination. Let's get together over the break and try to get ahead of this."

The words *deadly combination* stuck in her mind long after the call ended.

CHAPTER THREE

The March sun dipped below the horizon, leaving a kaleidoscope of pastels in the western sky. It was that magic time between sundown and night, the hour when the sky can't decide what it wants to wear, so it tries on everything in the closet. CJ looked beyond their neighbors' pool, down the bank, past the river and into cross-fenced fields of waving wheat and sleek cattle. The banks along the river of the thirty-seven-hundred-acre ranch wore their spring apparel of bluebonnets and Indian paintbrushes. She inhaled deeply, as if trying to breathe in the hues and shades.

David glanced across the poolside table, recently divested of food and plates. His gaze locked on a young man of eighteen with an unruly mop of black hair. "Randy, you've been quiet this evening. Is there something on your mind?"

"Huh? Oh, I'm sorry. What was that you said?"

Bea Stargate, CJ's friend, confidant, neighbor, and occasional therapist, joined the conversation. "David asked if something was eatin' on you. You haven't said three words since you got here."

Randy studied his shoes for a quiet couple of seconds,

then looked up and scanned the faces of those gathered around the table. He turned to the teenage girl sitting beside him. Nancy appeared ready to speak if he didn't.

"You might as well hear it from me first." Randy's voice caught, but soon recovered. "My dad's being released the day after tomorrow."

The news came as a surprise to CJ. "I thought he wasn't eligible for release until next fall."

"In his letter he said it had something to do with prison budget cuts and them releasing a bunch of non-violent offenders."

Billy Paul chimed in. "But your pa hurt some folks real bad in that car wreck. Doesn't that qualify as a violent crime?"

David answered for Randy. "They reduced the charges to felony DWI in a plea bargain agreement."

Billy Paul gave a short harrumph of disgust.

Bea reached for Randy's hand. "This isn't good news, is it?"

The teenage boy went back to studying his shoes. "No, ma'am."

"Ain't right," huffed Billy Paul.

CJ sounded a note of optimism, albeit guarded. "Perhaps the time your dad served in prison has changed him. I know they offer inmates drug and alcohol counseling. Do you know if he attended any of those?"

Randy shrugged. "This is the first I've heard from him since he got locked up." He squared his slumped shoulders. "This much I know—if he attended classes, he only did it to con the system so he could get out early."

Bea, the peacemaker, patted his hand and said, "Why don't you tell David what you and Mr. Bob have been up to?"

David made an educated guess. "Did you two find another old car to restore?"

As if someone had turned a light switch on, Randy's countenance lit up. "You didn't see it in your barn?"

David answered with a shake of his head. "What did Dad get this time?"

Randy beamed. "We found a '69 Pontiac GTO Judge."

David moved to the edge of his seat. "Didn't that come with a 400 cubic inch engine?"

"Mr. Bob is pricing a rebuilt one, but he may end up going with something newer."

David salivated. "Is that what you did over spring break? I wondered why Dad wasn't around."

"We went the day before spring break. Drove to Odessa to pick it up."

"Ahh," was the only response David made.

Bea looked at Nancy. "Tell us about your trip to South Padre Island."

"It was crazy good, but bad at the same time. I couldn't wait to get back. I missed little Davey so much."

"Tell us about the beach."

"It was awesome. There were tall sand dunes and waves big enough for surfing. The beach is on one side of the island and the Laguna Madre on the other. It looked just like it does on the Internet. Walking at dawn where the waves meet the seashore was my favorite."

"But?" CJ left the question open-ended.

Nancy leaned forward. "By noon the crowds were thick as the oatmeal you cooked last week."

That earned chuckles and nods of heads. CJ didn't dispute that her skills in culinary arts matched her lack of interest.

Nancy continued after flashing her a mischievous smile. "I think every college in the state dumped their students on the island. That's not counting those from other states and high school kids. Party, party, party. I never saw so much liquor and dope in my life."

"What were most of the kids into?" asked David.

"You name it, it was all there. But the thing that surprised me the most was moonshine."

"Moonshine?" David and CJ exchanged a look and leaned forward.

Nancy nodded. "I thought that stuff went out of style after Prohibition, but there it was. You could buy it almost anywhere and it came in plastic water bottles. Local kids were selling it up and down the beach to whoever had the money. They had water too, but mostly it was their *agua loco* that everyone wanted."

"Now that's interesting," said David with a far-off look.

Conversation took a brief respite, so Bea changed the subject. "Tell 'em about your new toys, Billy Paul."

A wide grin spread across his suntanned face. "Bought a new excavator and a couple of bigger front-end loaders for the rock quarry. They're better than anything we currently use and they'll cut down the time to load trucks and rail cars."

CJ marveled at how Billy Paul didn't fit the image of a Texas multi-millionaire. His normal attire consisted of overalls, a long sleeve shirt, a John Deere baseball cap, and scuffed work boots. Yet, he had vision and drive enough to take rocky, Central Texas land and make a fortune selling gravel, crushed stone, slabs and boulders. Many of the foundations of the state's roads came from his quarry.

Bea rose from her seat to put things away in the kitchen. Unspoken, it signaled the end of the meal and spring break. The men wandered away to carry on their talk of muscle cars and heavy equipment while the women drifted into the house to make quick work of returning the kitchen to its pre-dinner state of orderliness. At least that's what they told the men. CJ knew it was an opportunity for her and Bea to glean more information from Nancy about the trip to South Padre Island.

Bea, a professor of psychology, had an earthy, homespun way about her that caused students to open up and spill out information. CJ believed her techniques surpassed anything the FBI or CIA was capable of.

After ten minutes of small talk, Bea asked, "Did y'all see anyone get high real quick?"

CJ added, "Like almost instantly?"

Nancy pushed her lips to one side "Hmmm." Her face came back to normal. "Lindsey said she saw a guy give a girl a lollipop. She unwrapped it and gave it a lick. A few seconds later the girl started swaying and keeled over."

"Was she all right?" asked CJ.

"Lindsey didn't say, other than the girl was so messed up the lollipop fell in the sand. I think it was the moonshine the girl was drinking. Lindsey tasted it and said it was like drinking liquid fire."

Nancy looked toward the back door. "Davey needs a bath and so do I. Thanks, Aunt Bea. Dinner was awesome."

Bea gave Nancy a parting hug and sent her on her way. As the door closed, Bea opined, "One rots your liver and the other your teeth. Moonshine and lollipops."

CHAPTER FOUR

Anod of approval came from CJ as she passed heavy equipment gouging land that would be the sight of the new campus police station. She continued down the tree-lined road until she pulled into the parking lot of her current workplace, a Korean war-era military building converted into the ACU cop shop. She whispered a brief prayer that construction on the new building would progress without delays.

A telephone rang in the dispatcher's office as soon as she entered the lobby. She walked past the break room and smelled stale coffee. A step back to the doorway brought several discarded Styrofoam cups on the table into view. Nothing unusual for the first day back from spring break, but the lieutenants would need to remind their officers again to make sure they kept the area clean.

CJ turned down the hall toward her office, but John's voice stopped her mid-stride. She stepped toward his doorway. "Did you need something?"

John looked up from the papers on his desk and motioned

her to come in. "Maria should be here any minute. I wanted us to go over some things."

CJ settled in a chair. "Did you have trouble getting the girls out of bed this morning?"

"You'd think two fourth graders would know the routine by now, but spring break spoiled them. Dotty took the bugle off the shelf in my office and blew reveille. That did the trick."

The thought of her five-foot, two-inch former roommate at the Highway Patrol Academy blowing a wake-up call caused CJ to grin. "I forgot she played the trumpet in high school. Who could imagine that would come in handy in rearing children?"

CJ's thoughts turned to her job. "Did anything go on last night?"

"The usual—keys locked in cars, two front bicycle tires missing, and traffic stops. Nothing serious."

"No moonshine or fentanyl?"

A knock on the door preceded the entry of Maria Vasquez, the only detective of the small campus police force. CJ took a long look at Maria's bruised face. "Did you bob when you should have weaved?"

"He had a six-inch reach on me. It took a while to work through his defense."

The woman may have been diminutive, but there was nothing lacking in her ability to handle herself within the octagon of a mixed martial arts ring. She settled herself in a chair and asked, "Did I hear something about moonshine and fentanyl?"

"That's what we hoped you'd tell us," said John.

Wearing a knit shirt with the police logo on it, a thin windbreaker, skinny jeans and black tennis shoes, Maria crossed one leg over the other. "All the lab reports came back negative for fentanyl from the three girls partying with Holly

Grimes. The other student that went to the hospital did test positive, along with Holly. I put the word out with some students I'm in tight with to let me know if they hear anything about moonshine or fentanyl."

"I picked up something interesting from Nancy," said CJ. "She went to South Padre Island with three other girls. She said moonshine was being sold by kids on the beach. It came in water bottles, just like the ones we found in the dorm room. In fact, the kids had both water and moonshine to sell. She didn't know how the sellers could tell the difference."

"Probably something on the label," said Maria.

CJ nodded in agreement. "One more thing, and it might be nothing. Nancy said a girl who was drinking moonshine was licking a lollipop. She went down like a ton of bricks."

Maria's eyebrows raised. "Lollipop? Hold on." She grabbed her cell phone and started scrolling. "These are some photos I took when I first arrived at Holly's dorm room. Let me blow up this one."

John circled his desk as CJ rose and bent over to get a better view of the phone.

"There," said Maria. "In the trash. Isn't that a lollipop?"

"I can't tell," said John. "Was it collected as evidence?"

Maria hung her head. "It was in the bathroom, nowhere near Holly." She swallowed. "I'm sorry."

John returned to his desk. "Go back and talk to the girls that were with Holly in the dorm. Ask if they remember a lollipop."

Maria nodded.

With that subject put to bed, John said, "Holly's funeral is tomorrow." He looked at CJ. "One of us needs to go."

"I hate funerals for students, but it makes sense for me to go since I already know the family. Besides, I can ride with David. He has some sort of meeting in Killeen." CJ looked at her phone. "Don't you have a class to teach?"

John glanced up at a wall clock. "Two classes. One at ten and another at eleven. Then, I need to check on our new building. We're having to change some things to make the building more green."

CJ rose. "That leaves me cooped up in my office most of the day. I'm going to the Campus Grind while I can. Do you want to come along, Maria?"

"No, I'm good. I'll track down the girls that were partying with Holly and check with some of my sources about the moonshine and fentanyl."

"And I'll ask Yari while I'm at the Grind."

A WOODEN BENCH under a live oak tree served as a place for CJ to pull out her cell phone and give David a call. After six rings, she received instructions to leave a message. "Hey. I wanted to let you know you'll have a passenger tomorrow. I'm going to Holly's funeral. I don't think you told me what meeting you were going to in Killeen, but you can drop me off somewhere." She looked up to see a squirrel less than four feet away, perched on its hind legs, looking straight at her as if she were trespassing. "Call me when you can. Nothing much happening on campus. No more moonshine or fentanyl."

She slid her phone back into her jacket pocket and rose. "King Squirrel, I apologize for entering your realm."

The apology must have been sufficient. The squirrel scurried away, scaled the tree and looked down at her from a lofty perch.

CJ crisscrossed the campus, alternately dodging the ambling students and getting out of the way of those late for class. She pulled open the door of the Campus Grind, the epicenter of campus life and the home of strong coffee and mouth-watering sweets. It took all her willpower to abstain from an apple fritter and be content with a large coffee. As expected, Bea Stargate waved CJ over to her usual table where students came and went with regularity.

"You missed Nancy," said Bea as CJ took a seat that gave her an excellent view of the room swirling with students coming and going. "Got herself an espresso, so she'd be good and alert for her lab. Rumor has it there'll be a test on Friday for what they're supposed to learn in class today. She didn't want to be blindsided."

"She's a smart girl," said CJ as she looked around. "Most of them are busy retelling tales of spring break."

"It'll take 'em a couple of days to get back in the groove. That's why I don't give tests the first week back."

Bea's gaze shifted, and her perpetual smile widened. "Look who's comin' bearing gifts."

Approaching their table was a woman wearing a chef's uniform and mismatched tennis shoes. Her hair was a soft lavender color, and she was about the same age as CJ. She carried two small white paper sacks. "There goes the diet," said CJ.

"Hey, CJ. Hey, Bea. I made something new for you to try. It's a take-off on biscotti. Tell me what you think."

CJ pulled out the crispy baked treat, put it on the sack, and gave it a good look-over.

Bea didn't wait. She removed hers and took a bite that gave a crackle. Then she moaned and spoke before she swallowed. "Lord, have mercy, Yari. There's a half-dozen flavors doing the two-step in my mouth."

With head lowered to examine it from a different angle, CJ said, "I've never seen biscotti with chocolate icing on the bottom and white chocolate on the top."

"The students like things sweet," said Yari. "Did you notice the almond slivers?"

"I couldn't miss them."

By now, Bea had swallowed her first bite. "The little orange-colored flecks inside don't taste like an orange or a tangerine. What are they?"

"Finely minced apricots," said Yari. "I wanted to try something different."

Bea kept asking questions about Yari's latest creation while CJ scanned the room. She leaned into Bea. "Isn't that Amy Sneller talking to that preppy looking young man?"

Bea eased her gaze around the room and stopped when she found the students in question. She looked at Yari and said, "Move a little to the left, honey. I don't want Amy to know I'm looking at her." After Yari moved, Bea looked past her and then directed her gaze back to Yari. "Have you ever seen Amy Sneller talk to anyone here?"

Yari shook her head. "Never."

"Is she still selling pot?" asked CJ.

Yari sat down across from Bea. "I'm out of the loop now that I'm on probation. When I kept my ear to the ground, she had an organization that ran three or four deep. She's too smart to sell anything herself."

CJ looked at Bea. "What do you know about her?"

"She was in my Christian ethics class three years ago. She'd argue with a fence post if she couldn't find anyone else to take on. Real bright, but as dedicated an atheist as you'll ever find. The only reason she's here is because she's a legacy. Her grandmother went here, and this is the only free ride Amy could get. The last I heard, she's working on a master's in political science. I believe she wants to go on and get a doctorate."

"She can't get that here," said CJ.

Yari added, "I'd look for her to go someplace on either of the coasts where the schools aren't so conservative."

"Or Moscow," said Bea with a chuckle.

CJ stole a glance back to where Amy sat. "Who's that guy she's talking to?"

Yari stood. "I'll find out."

Absentmindedly, CJ took a bite of her biscotti. "Oh, my gosh. That's incredible."

Bea nodded, but didn't speak because her mouth was busy chewing.

CJ glanced toward Amy again and saw a look of irritation narrowing her eyebrows. She spoke with teeth gritted and pointed toward the door. The young man grinned as he strolled to the door and left the building.

Amy turned on her heel and stalked toward the side door, pushing harder than necessary to open it.

Yari returned, this time bearing information instead of treats. "His name is Peter Starks. He's a junior transfer student from some college in North Carolina. Stacy says he has a sexy accent and awesome clothes. She goes for the preppy ones."

"Starks." CJ shook her head. "He's not on our radar."

The jangle of CJ's phone ended the conversation with Bea and Yari.

"I won't need to drop you off anywhere," said David. "You can come with me. I already have you approved."

"Approved? For what?"

"A meeting at the Bell County Sheriff's office. There's an uptick in fentanyl OD's, especially among soldiers at Fort Hood."

"What about moonshine?"

"They didn't mention it." He paused. "I also arranged for us to take off a few days."

"You did? Where are we going?"

"It's a surprise."

<hr>

CHAPTER FIVE

<hr>

Fluorescent light illuminated a patch of gravel outside David and CJ's barn as David brought his SUV to a stop. He exited, flipped the door shut, and tried to stretch away a day's worth of work, stress, and tedium. The so-called status of wearing the badge was more myth than truth. More time was spent being chased by paperwork and meetings than chasing desperadoes. Metal clanking preceded a muffled expression of derision. He stepped into the brightness of overhead lights and halogen work lights mounted on floor stands.

"Working late, Dad?"

"I'm trying to wrestle in a new drive shaft and universal joint."

"Randy couldn't help you tonight?"

"He left about thirty minutes ago. Still working three nights a week at the university as a janitor." Another groan of effort came from under the car. "By the way, Randy's sporting a new busted lip. A present from his father."

"Uh-oh. That's not good."

Bob gave a final grunt. "There, that's all I can do tonight."

He gave a firm tug with greasy hands on the frame of the geri-atric Pontiac and squirted out from under it. He paused as he lay on the back of a creeper, a board with four wheels and a padded head rest that rose about two inches off the concrete floor. The extension of his hand was Bob's invitation for his son to help him to his feet. David did so and then viewed the smudge of some foreign substance that must have found its way to the GTO's belly when Nixon was president.

"Don't worry. It'll wash off."

David grabbed a shop towel and got most of it on the first swipe, but smeared the rest. As he rubbed, he stated the obvi-ous. "What's bothering you?"

The elder man resettled a filthy baseball cap on his head, covering all the brown and leaving only a ring of silver. "Nothing."

"Oh?"

It was one of those quick questions that might elicit a non-committal "none-of-your-business," or could open the door to a long tête-à-tête.

"Sit down with me. We need to have a talk."

Father and son each arranged a lawn chair at the barn's door so they faced the pasture overlooking the river. David sat silently until his father began the conversation. The mind of the mechanical engineer needed to have things in order.

"Are you concerned about the way McNutt Sr. is treating Randy?"

"That's part of it."

"What else?"

"It's not only what happened with Randy, but what might happen at the university." Bob paused, then spoke into the night. "Alice had a meeting with the board of regents yester-day. Some are pushing for long range planning that will, and I quote, 'Bring about systemic changes in the university's direc-tion to better meet the needs of an ever-changing society.'"

"What does that mean in English?"

"It's code for a desire to transform Agape Christian University into what you see in so many other schools."

David thought about the implications, how they would affect CJ and, especially, Alice. "When did you say the board of regents met?"

"Yesterday. The meeting went into the night."

David remained silent, allowing his father to give more details.

"Things got heated and personal."

Father and son looked into each other's eyes, and Bob continued in a voice laced with not-so-mild sarcasm. "Some members think ACU needs fresh direction to compete in today's high-tech world. You know, the standard line of bull. I called Billy Paul to find out what really happened."

Bob turned toward the river again and made an observation. "I didn't know Billy Paul could get so angry."

David waited for his father to get back on track.

"Anyway, he came over and told me face to face. It seems there's a move to squeeze Alice out, and it's coming from two directions. One coalition wants the university to transition to a more secular stance in order to attract additional government funding. A second group, let's call them the hyper-conservatives, doesn't like the optics of Alice seeing an ex-con." He paused. "Then, there's a third group headed by Billy Paul that's in Alice's corner."

David gave a nod to show he understood the dilemma Alice faced. "Was anything decided?"

Bob shook his head. "Seven hours of back-and-forth bickering and nothing happened but a lot of bruised egos and hard feelings." He sighed.

"How did Alice take it?" asked David.

Bob rearranged his hat once more. "It hurt her, hurt her

bad. She's dedicated her heart and soul to that university. But you know Alice. She's putting on a good front."

"What are her chances of getting fired?"

"Billy Paul isn't sure. It's a three-way split now, but a lot can happen in politics."

David turned away and looked into the blackness of a moonless night outside the barn. "Something like students dying from drug or alcohol overdose?"

"That might do it."

After David took a step toward the open sliding barn door, Bob said, "Wait, Son. There's one more thing."

David spun. "Yeah?"

"It's time for me to find a place to live on my own. Your travel trailer is a blessing, but—"

David finished the thought. "But for someone they locked up for sixteen years, you've had enough of living in a small space. I was wondering how long it would take before the walls of that trailer started closing in on you. Now that you've gotten your restitution from the State there's no reason for you not to have your own place."

"You know I appreciate all you and CJ have done for me, but I think it's time."

"It's been good having you here." David hugged his dad. "You'll still be using the barn for your restoration business, won't you?"

"If you don't mind. I also enjoy being available for little Davey and Nancy."

"Our barn is your barn."

"Thanks." Bob pointed in the house's direction. "Walk lightly when you go in. CJ's not a happy camper."

DAVID DIDN'T BOTHER MOVING his vehicle under the carport. After bidding his father good night, he shuffled past the pool and scaled two steps up to the back porch. A turn of the knob and the back door swung smoothly on its hinges. He stood in the breakfast nook overlooking the kitchen, trying to catch the scent of what might have been for supper. Either they completely consumed it or, more likely, placed the remnants in plastic bowls on the second shelf of the refrigerator.

David kicked off his boots, then padded his way down the hallway to their bedroom, footwear in hand.

"There you are," he said. "I thought I might catch you watching a movie. Where's Nancy? Is there anything to eat?"

CJ sat upright in bed, legs crossed, one pillow in her lap supporting a magazine and three more pillows stuffed between her back and the headboard. She ignored the first comment about a movie, and barked out, "Nancy's on a farm call with Doc Steel. There's Hamburger Helper in the Cool Whip bowl on the second shelf. Help yourself."

She went back to abusing the magazine by slapping from one page to the next. "Are you just now coming in from the barn? I heard you drive up thirty minutes ago."

"Is it my imagination, or is it a little chilly in here tonight?"

CJ tossed the magazine at him and let out a "Grrrrrr."

As David beat a retreat, he quipped, "I'm going to grab a bite to eat. Do you want me to bring you a bone to gnaw on?"

Silence.

"By the way, I've been with Dad. He told me about it."

David bypassed the Hamburger Helper and went for cold chicken and a glass of milk. CJ made a not-so-grand appearance on his third bite of thigh and gave him a firm behind the back hug.

"What can we do to help Randy?" asked CJ.

David swallowed and shrugged. "Don't know there's anything we can do. We have to wait and see how things play out."

"How can you be so insensitive?"

"Randy can go to the sheriff's office and swear out a complaint whenever he wants. Or, he can move out."

She mounted the barstool next to him and scowled.

David raised the chicken thigh, but didn't take a bite. "Randy's perfectly capable of finding a place to rent. I'd say the best thing we can do is stay out of his way and let him make an adult decision."

He took a bite and talked while he chewed. "As for Dad, that goes double for him."

"What are you talking about?"

David stopped chewing. "Didn't you know Dad wants to move out of the trailer?"

"I thought you'd been talking to him about that stupid car. He's moving out?"

"Yeah, and knowing him, it will be as soon as he can."

CJ's cheeks puffed out and then reduced to normal as she blew out. "I've been home four hours and I have to learn from you what's going on in my backyard. Is there any other crisis I need to know about?"

David cleaned the bone, shoved the meat to one side and mumbled, "Other than what's going on with Alice?"

She threw up her hands. "Alice? What about Alice?"

David stopped chewing, tried to swallow, but got choked. He wondered if the intention behind the swift blows between his shoulder blades was to heal or harm. Either way, they did the trick. After he recovered, he relayed the conversation concerning Alice's predicament.

CJ sat stone faced with wide eyes until he finished, then issued a much-used reply. "Good grief."

"My sentiments exactly."

Her long hair swung as she gave her head a slow turn from side to side. "I can't imagine the university with someone else as president."

David muffled a burp with his napkin. "If I was a betting man, I'd wager names are being floated around as her replacement."

CJ grabbed a handful of hair with each fist, gave both a firm tug and stomped away with a loud, "AAARG!"

CHAPTER SIX

The next morning, David watched as his father ran a dishtowel down the throat of his favorite coffee mug and placed the freshly washed ceramic treasure in its place, the cabinet over an undersized sink. He glanced left and then right and took in everything from stem to stern of the place he called home, a thirty-two-foot-long fifth-wheel travel trailer cocooned within the barn. "Be it ever so humble." Bob took two steps to the living room to retrieve his cell phone. He checked the caller ID, put it on speaker and issued a cheerful, "Good morning, Billy Paul."

"Mornin'. Got your britches on?"

"Since first light. I've been on the internet trying to find a place to lease. Not much luck. I may have to camp out here until I can build something. David and CJ talked it over last night and they're cutting out five acres for me to build on up by the road."

Billy Paul, with his usual economy of words, sailed on. "I'm heading over to get ya'. There's a place I think might do for a while. I called Bea. She's meeting us there in thirty minutes."

"Great, I'll be waiting for you."

David followed in his SUV. Three blocks past the university, Billy Paul's one-ton Dodge truck made a left turn, traveled two blocks, and rested in the shade of a massive pecan tree. This was an area euphemistically called Old Town, a quadrant of homes that came with wide, wrap-around front porches. They were built by workers who knew the meaning of the word craft. Those tradesman earned every penny of the wages paid by yesteryear's doctors, judges, and university professors.

Once on the sidewalk, Bob said, "This is quite a shack. What's the story on it?"

"Belongs to an engineer that's living in China for another nine months."

"The house is empty?"

Billy Paul looked down the street to see Bea's Mercedes SUV approach with Alice in the passenger's seat. CJ followed behind in a university patrol car.

"Good," said Billy Paul. "Let's wait on the gals."

Bea spoke loud enough to be heard by all. "Alice, CJ, look. There's three of the most handsome men I ever saw. I'll take that one on the left home with me." She pointed a finger at Billy Paul.

Alice joined Bob while CJ took David's arm and said, "Looks like you're stuck with me."

David smiled. "I think I can handle that."

The three couples gazed down a thirty-yard sidewalk to a three-story white Queen Ann Victorian.

Alice's gaze drank in the 1920s creation. "Billy Paul, this is fabulous, but it's way too much house for Bob. It would take a small fortune to fill it with furniture."

"That's one of the reasons I thought this would be the perfect place for Bob. The house is fully furnished, or at least enough for Bob to live in."

Bea took over. "Frank and his wife bought this place for a song and it needed a ton of love. They don't have kids, so this place is their baby. They got the downstairs finished, the outside painted, a new pool put in the backyard, and took care of their bedroom and bath. Then, this opportunity to go to China popped up. The renovation came to a halt, and they stored all their personal belongings upstairs, hoping they'd eventually find someone to house sit for them."

"And they're willing to lease it for nine months?" asked Bob.

"Not exactly," said Billy Paul.

Bea jumped in again. "When Billy Paul called them and told them Bob was in a bind for a place to live, they said he would be an answer to their prayers. They were afraid something bad might happen to the house with it being empty for so long. All they want is for Bob to house sit, take care of any repairs that might pop up, and send them the bill. You can't lease it, but you can have it for free; well, almost free. You'll need to take care of utility payments and trash pickup."

"Let's look inside, before you decide," said Billy Paul.

Bob admired the craftsmanship. Alice moaned with pleasure as she took in the choices of muted colors chosen for each room's paint. Coordinating colors framed each double-paned window, and all the trim work.

Bea and Billy Paul exchanged nods when Bob and Alice played the 'This could be,' game. One room after another Alice announced, "This could be your office, and this could be a place for a drafting table." She mentally arranged furniture in each space and spoke out loud as she did so.

David pulled CJ into another room and whispered. "Is she arranging this house for him, or them?"

CJ put a hand over her mouth to suppress a giggle. "Wouldn't that be a hoot?"

They rejoined the group, and the tour clicked along without a hitch.

Alice approached the kitchen counter, grabbed it with both hands and, in a most uncharacteristic display of emotions, fell apart. Tears coursed down her cheeks as she heaved sobs.

Bea exclaimed, "Alice, what's wrong? We thought this might be the perfect solution, but it's fine if it's not."

Bob draped an arm over Alice's shoulders. "No, no, it's perfect. It's just been a stressful few days lately."

He gave Alice's shoulders a squeeze and looked at Billy Paul. "If you'll give me Frank's email address, I'll tell him he has a customer."

AN HOUR AFTER SUNSET, the knock on the back door caught both CJ and Nancy by surprise. Nancy rose from the table in the breakfast nook, leaving behind an open *INTRODUCTION TO CHEMISTRY* textbook and a journal with a spiral metal spine. She walked barefoot to the door, flipped on the porch light and gazed through the glass. She gave the knob a quick clockwise twist.

"Randy, what are you doing here?"

When CJ saw the young man's face, she knew. The welt on his right eye was red and angry, but not as angry as Randy. His narrow-eyed-gaze did the talking for him. He stepped inside, holding a dishtowel on his left arm. The stain on it looked like red Kool-Aid, but CJ knew it was blood.

Nancy nudged him to a chair and scraped away pens, papers, and a textbook with her forearm until they were out of harm's way. Ever so gently, she pulled back the dishtowel to examine the gash.

"This is going to need stitches."

Randy's words came forth with conviction. "I ain't going to no hospital."

The sound of little Davey's hands slapping the floor signaled his arrival in the kitchen. He crawled toward Randy, and gave his assessment of the situation in nine-month-old terms.

Nancy confirmed the diagnosis. "Yes, Randy has an 'owie.'"

As if shot from a cannon, the toddler spun on his diaper and crawled away.

It wasn't long before another voice came their way. Bob walked into the kitchen area speaking baby talk with Davey. As they rounded the corner CJ moved to Davey, took the tike, and settled him on her hip. Nancy's thin frame hid the bleeding arm.

CJ gave a quick nod to her father-in-law. "We have a patient."

Nancy washed her hands and returned. "Let's look at that eye first." She tilted his chin toward the light. "That doesn't look too bad. You'll need to put ice on it as soon as you can. Did you lose consciousness? Do you have a headache?"

"No. He only tagged me once, and not that hard."

"It doesn't appear he has a concussion, but we better get it checked," said Nancy. "I'm used to looking at cattle, dogs, and cats, not knuckleheads."

She turned back to Randy. "You'll have a nice shiner for a few days that will turn green, yellow and all kinds of cool colors."

She stood up straight. "Before I look at that arm, I'll get my bag."

"Do you need gloves?" asked CJ.

"Doc Steel bought me a backpack and filled it with all kinds of things for emergency farm calls. He wanted me to have what I needed to grab and go at a moment's notice. I've got gloves that go to the shoulder, if I need them."

Nancy returned, rewashed her hands, and slipped on a pair of exam gloves. "Let's check the damage."

"How did this happen?" asked Bob.

Randy's lips pursed shut, but Nancy's words spilled out. "I can tell you how this happened. His daddy got drunk and took a knife to him."

Removal of the dishtowel revealed a substantial slice in the sleeve of a cotton shirt and more blood oozing from a half-hidden wound.

"I'll need scissors to cut away this sleeve."

Bob moved to the backpack and slid a pair out of a pocket.

Nancy pointed. "Look inside. There's a box of gauze pads and tape that I'll need."

Quick snips took care of the blood-soaked shirtsleeve and revealed a diagonal gash, about five inches long running from shoulder to bicep.

CJ took a step forward and spoke without thinking. "That's worse than I thought."

Bob extended his hands to little Davey, still straddling CJ's hip. "I think I'll take this buckaroo out of the operating room."

"Good grief," said CJ. "I forgot I was carrying him. Take him into our bedroom. There's another episode of Baby Einstein cued up."

Nancy examined Randy's cut again. "You're going to need a bunch of stitches. I'll dress it so you won't make too big of a mess on your way to the ER."

Randy bristled. "I'm not going to any hospital to get stitched up."

Nancy stood her ground, "Oh, yes, you are."

"No, I ain't."

Volume increased.

"Yes, you are!"

"No, I ain't!"

David stepped through the back door with a scowl painted across his face. His gaze fixed on Randy and passed from face to bleeding arm. Bending over, he placed his hands on his knees and moved to within inches of Randy's nose.

"Did your father hit you and cut you?"

"Yes, sir."

"Do you want your dad to go to jail tonight?"

"No, sir."

"Tough. Assault with a deadly weapon is a felony. He made the decision for you."

Randy nodded. "I'm pretty sure he's still out cold."

"You hit him back?"

"Right after he cut me, I decked him."

"Uh-huh. Why don't you want to get stitched up?"

"He stole all my money and filled his liquor cabinet. I can't afford to see a doctor."

Nancy came unhinged. "Randy McNutt Junior. You're the most pig-headed jackass that ever drew a breath. You're sitting in a room full of people who would give you the shirt off their backs, let alone chip in and see you got a few stitches." She apparently ran low on insults and made do with a none-too-gentle slap across the back of his head.

Randy looked up at the girl whose red face competed with her hair and said sheepishly, "I thought you might sew me up. You have everything you need in your vet kit, don't you?"

David straightened his back and covered his mouth with his hand. He drew it downward over his chin as if to drain the frustration.

CJ attempted to diffuse the tension in the room with soft words. "It's not that simple, Randy. The wound needs to be cleaned thoroughly with special soaps to kill the germs.

There may be muscle damage that will require stitches below the top layer. Proper sterile bandages will need to be applied after the wound is closed and you'll need a tetanus shot. Nancy can't do that here."

Nancy wasn't nearly so kind. "Or I could pour kerosene on it, give you a roll of duct tape, and tell you to do the best you can."

David had another question for his wife. "Are all of Dad's things out of the trailer?"

"We have the last load in the old pickup. He planned on leaving earlier, but wanted to discuss building his new house with you."

"Good," said David. He leaned toward Randy with his hands again on his knees. "Young man, you had a bad day? So did I."

CJ closed her eyes. Uh-oh. Here it comes.

David began speaking softly, but the volume increased each time he took a breath. "My day started in a hallway outside a courtroom waiting to be called as the prosecution's witness in a rape case. I worked six months on that case. I did everything by the book and presented an air-tight case to the district attorney's office. Do you know what happened? I'll tell you what happened. Some clerk forgot to subpoena the prosecution's witnesses. Not all, mind you, only the most important ones, the forensics expert and the examining physician. The assistant district attorney didn't have sense enough to ask for postponement and tried to wing it. Without the foundation of medical evidence, the defense cleaned my clock, and a dangerous man is walking free as we speak."

David's gaze shifted from person to person. "Do you know where I spent this afternoon and evening? After I got reamed out by my boss for not double checking with the DA to make sure they did the job they're paid to do, I had the pleasure of going to six women and explaining to them why the man that violated them is back on the street. I also told them they might want to check their locks and buy a can of pepper spray."

He lowered his voice and gave Randy an icy glare. "And now I find you here, dripping blood on my floor and telling everyone you don't want to get stitches. Well, Mr. Randy McNutt Junior, I'm going to tell you what's going to happen. CJ is going to give Nancy a credit card. Nancy will take you to Riverview Regional Medical Center, where a nice doctor is going to sew you up. While you're there, a deputy will come and take a statement from you."

David took a step back. "Then, you and Nancy are going to Walmart where she'll buy what you need for one week. That includes seven changes of clothes, toiletries, food, and anything else she can think of." He reached into his back pocket, pulled out his wallet and withdrew a stack of bills. "This is your spending money until you get paid again. Dad's out of the trailer and you're in. This feud between you and your dad ends tonight. Tomorrow morning you and I are going to your dad's place, where you'll have one chance to get everything that belongs to you. Questions?"

"No sir, except I don't need to go there in the morning. I grabbed everything that's mine and threw it in the trunk of my car before I left."

"That's the first sensible thing I've heard from you tonight."

David addressed Nancy. "Can you patch him up enough so he won't get blood all over his car?"

"Can do."

"Good. I'm going to bed."

"Uh, honey..." said CJ. "Your dad and little Davey are in there watching Baby Einstein."

"That's fine. I'll relieve Dad and unload my troubles on someone who won't remember what I say."

CJ, accompanied by Sandy, her faithful four-legged shadow, entered the bedroom. After surveying the scene, she scooped Davey in her arms. Sandy gave David's hand a lick, received an ear rub and trotted to catch up with CJ and Davey who waited at the door.

After placing little Davey in his bed, CJ padded her way back to their bedroom and entered the walk-in closet. She exited wearing a football jersey and sleep shorts, her version of pajamas. Slipping between the sheets, she nestled into a pillow and whispered, "Love you."

"Mmmm."

CHAPTER SEVEN

Green interstate mile markers clicked by as David shifted in the driver's seat. CJ rode shotgun. He glanced at her, but she didn't react. "Still mad?"

"Not much."

"That means you are. Want to talk about it?"

"You said what you wanted to say, and I did the same. There's nothing left to discuss."

"I still say you shouldn't have sent Nancy out to the trailer with Randy's breakfast. He can come to the house or fix his own. No need to baby him."

CJ swiveled as best she could to turn away from him. "Drop it."

"Fine."

"Yeah. Fine."

More miles passed in silence.

"Did Nancy give you the receipts for the hospital and everything they bought at Walmart?" he asked.

"I put them on your desk."

"Thanks."

No reply.

David noted the never-ending construction in Temple as they drove past at fifty-five miles per hour. "Do you think they'll ever finish building roads?"

CJ shrugged. "There's a travel center a few miles ahead. I need a pit stop."

He nodded. "Why did you get so mad at me?"

CJ tried to count to ten but only made it to five. "It's obvious you won't let this rest, so I'll tell you. You see yourself in Randy and want him to act like you think he should. He's not you. He acts and reacts differently."

David kept his eyes on the road. "Life's hard. Randy isn't a helpless child. He's a man and should start acting like one."

"Says you."

"Yeah, says me."

"Fine."

"Fine!"

Even though the signs for the travel center were many and bold enough to capture the attention of even the most distracted drivers, David almost missed the exit. He braked hard and came close to side-swiping a green Chevy Volt. Instead of saying anything, CJ braced herself for impact and kept her gaze fixed straight ahead.

David stayed in the SUV while CJ went in. The tiny green car he'd almost sent into a ditch pulled next to him. A red-faced woman exited the car and gave him a tongue-lashing that ranked number four in the top five he'd ever received. He'd earned those, too. After she left, David slammed his door and paced beside the vehicle.

CJ returned with two cups of coffee. She placed them on the hood of the SUV, stepped backed until she stood on the curb, and motioned him to come toward her.

He did, which placed both of them at about the same height.

"Shut your eyes," she said in a tone that didn't invite dissension.

He stuffed his hands in the pockets of his cowboy-cut slacks and closed his eyes.

She grabbed the lapels of his sports coat and pulled him in. Lips touched. Arms enfolded him and if he wasn't so shocked, he'd have responded without opening his eyes. After receiving a toe-curling kiss, she pushed him back to arm's length.

CJ wasn't smiling. "You didn't deserve that kiss any more than Randy deserved breakfast being brought to him this morning. Now do you get it?"

He grinned. "I'm a slow learner. How 'bout we plan some remedial classes?"

Her smile returned. "That's exactly what I have planned for this mini-vacation you're taking me on tomorrow. Tell me where we're going."

"Pack light, bring a bathing suit and sunblock. That's all you need to know."

She grabbed her coffee. "That's plenty for now."

With their relationship back on an even keel, they traveled on to Killeen, parked in the side lot of a large Baptist church, and went inside. Many students from ACU skipped classes to attend the funeral, including the three who'd partied with Holly. Alice and Bob drove up with Bea and Billy Paul and sat near the family. The church continued to fill until ushers brought in extra folding chairs, lined the side aisles, and made two rows in the back.

David's mind drifted back in time to other funerals he'd attended. His mother's remained the one etched in his memory in all caps and bold lettering. After that, he recalled the empty boots of fallen soldiers. Then, his mind went to a few classmates who died in high school. Except for his mother, the too-brief lives of the children, teens and young adults seemed the most tragic and had the unenviable distinction of being the best attended funerals. Grief among teens burned the brightest. Their grief was loud today, but would be short-lived compared to the grief of Holly's parents.

Musings ceased when CJ took David's hand and urged him to his feet. She held open a hymnal and sang a song of benediction without looking at the words. He realized he'd been so lost in the past that he missed the pastor's mini-sermon. He'd tuned out after the eulogies.

The motorcade to the cemetery was exceptionally long and moved at a pace that never exceeded twenty miles per hour. Finally, he and CJ parked and found a place to stand where they could see the grieving parents with their arms around a teenage boy and a girl who looked to be in middle school. David noted a bearded man, also seated in the shade of the white tent reserved for the family. Something about him looked familiar, but the distance prohibited identification.

The overcast day came with mixed blessings of moderate temperatures but high humidity. As usual, the graveside service was relatively short, but filled with tears. Mourners passed by the family, and some touched the casket and mouthed last goodbyes. David took another look at the man seated behind Holly's father. The dark beard did a good job of hiding his face, as nervous eyes shifted from one person in line to the next. He stopped tugging on his collar as his eyes locked on David. It seemed as if each were trying to determine where he'd seen the other before. Then, a smile tugged up the corners of the man's mouth and he issued a lazy hand salute, like a soldier did out of obligation.

"Pancho Grimes," whispered David.

CJ's hand on his back propelled him to take a step and walk past the casket. They joined Alice, Bob, Bea, and Billy Paul in a clearing, away from the crowd. For several minutes they chatted about nothing. Then he saw Pancho headed toward them.

"Sergeant Harper." The voice boomed across the cemetery and caused heads to turn. "What brings you here?"

Pancho had him in a bear-hug before he could respond.

"Pancho, let me introduce you to some folks." After names and titles, David continued, "Pancho was in my company before he got a ticket home courtesy of a medivac helicopter and a hospital transport plane to Germany."

Billy Paul went for a second handshake. "Thank you for your service, Pancho. I take it you're kin to Holly?"

Pancho's countenance darkened. "Her uncle." He looked toward the gravesite. "She didn't deserve to die like this."

Billy Paul nodded in agreement.

Pancho's speech had a hesitation and a slur to his words. The close-cropped hair did nothing to hide the scar that ran from his temple to the back of his skull. David relived the IED explosion, the death of another soldier, and thinking there was no way Pancho would survive. But he did.

Pancho grabbed David by the arm and led him away from the group. "Did you say that pretty lady you're married to is the assistant chief of police at that college Holly went to?"

"That's right."

"Does she know who supplied the dope that killed Holly?"

"Not yet, but we're working on it."

Both of Pancho's eyes didn't focus on the same spot, making it difficult for David to know which one to concentrate on.

"What do you mean, 'we'?" asked Pancho.

David pulled back his coat enough so Pancho could see the badge pinned to his white shirt. "I'm still a sergeant, but I'm with the highway patrol assigned to help the Rangers."

Pancho took a step back, smiled, and then came forward.

"You let me know who supplied the dope that killed Holly and there won't need to be a trial."

With a hand resting on Poncho's shoulder, David said, "Nobody knows yet, and that's the truth. Besides, you know I always go by the book. I don't violate rules of engagement."

To get away from any talk of revenge, David asked, "What are you doing now?"

"I have a backhoe and I'll set septic tanks now and then. The sun gives me headaches, so mainly I get by on what the VA pays me. I like to hunt and fish more than anything."

"Around Waco?"

His head moved side to side with vigor. "Deep East Texas. Out a way from Ore City."

Billy Paul came to where they stood. "CJ told me to come get you. Said she's hungry and wants to eat at Cracker Barrel before your meeting."

David's gaze shifted between Pancho and Billy Paul. "It just occurred to me that you two have something in common. You both dig in the ground."

"You don't say," said Billy Paul. "Run on, David. Bea and Alice said we're going back to the church with the family. Pancho and I can talk about holes in the ground."

After he handed Pancho a business card, the two former soldiers hugged and parted. CJ met David halfway to his SUV. "I told your dad, Alice, and Bea we need to hit the road if we want to make it to the meeting on time." She spoke in muted tones as they walked to their vehicle. "Pancho's wounds were serious?"

"He shouldn't be alive."

"And Holly should be. Doesn't seem right, does it?"

"A lot of things aren't right in the world today. It seems like too many."

CJ waited until they got back into the SUV and the air conditioner was blowing before she continued the conversation. "I'm having a hard time thinking about anything but our trip. Give me another hint of where we're going."

David wiggled his eyebrows. "Imagine warm sand between your toes, water that's so blue and clear you can't believe it's real, and sunsets dipped in pure gold."

"Yum! Am I on a balcony watching the sunset?"

"Right beside me."

"Double yum."

CJ DOODLED on a yellow legal pad and tried to act interested as a captain from Fort Hood's Military Police Brigade gave a mind-numbing recitation of statistics for drug and alcohol abuse. He followed it by cataloging the programs and services available to soldiers and their families. Only after repeated questioning did he admit fentanyl abuse was on the rise. Similar reports of opioid abuse came from representatives of the Killeen Police Department and a handful of other law enforcement agencies. Between the emotionally draining funeral, the meal of down-home country cooking at one of her favorite restaurants, and a yawn-producing meeting, she wanted nothing more than to leave, go home, throw her toiletries into a suitcase, and switch to vacation mode.

She was drawing a picture of a seahorse when David stood. "Does anyone know how people are taking the fentanyl?"

The question earned many blank stares, but the army captain, not one to lack for words, said, "We believe they're mixing it with cocaine or heroin."

"There could be another form of delivery," said David. "When I was serving in the Middle East, Air Force medics sometimes used fentanyl in lollipops on severe combat causalities. They'd tape the stick to two fingers and place the candy in the soldier's mouth. After receiving enough, the hand would go limp and pull out the lollipop."

CJ jerked her head up. "You didn't tell me."

Smirks and giggles filtered across the room. CJ stood to explain. "David and I have just come from the funeral of an ACU student. She OD'd on fentanyl. There's a possibility the lethal dose was administered on or in a lollipop."

David looked at her with raised eyebrows.

Before he could ask a question, she said. "It's only a theory we're working on. The lollipop wasn't near the body, and it was long gone before we realized it was important."

She added, "We had one other student wind up in the hospital because of fentanyl, but her father's an attorney and told her not to talk to us."

Sympathetic heads nodded.

The captain spoke again. "We have about twenty-four thousand soldiers, plus their spouses and dependents. If the dealers are lacing lollipops with that stuff, we may have a wave of overdoses like we've never seen before. I'm especially concerned that kids may get hold of it by accident."

The room went quiet as CJ took her seat. David remained standing and said, "From what I've heard today, this situation deserves a special task force. I'll report what we discussed to Captain Crow. I suggest we all start gathering intel from whatever sources we have. If everyone knows what to look for, we'll find out soon enough if this is a blip on the radar or something much bigger."

The sheriff of Bell County stood as David took his seat. "If there's no objection, I'd like us to meet back here in one week. In the meantime, work your informants. This stuff is deadly. We need to find out who's behind it."

As the group dispersed, the loquacious army captain came to where CJ stood. The shine on his shoes was bright enough to reflect the light from the overhead lights. His youth became more apparent the closer he came.

"I'm glad you could come today, ma'am. I hoped I'd get to meet you before I received my next duty assignment. You have quite a reputation."

CJ raised her eyebrows. "Telling a woman she has quite a reputation could get you in trouble in today's army, Captain."

Blood rose from his neck and didn't stop until it reached his short, blond hairline. "I'm... Uh... I didn't mean—"

Her laugh and hand on his shoulder stopped him from tripping over any more words. "No need to apologize; I'm having fun at your expense. It's what cops do."

The look of abject fear melted away. Even his erect posture eased a little. He glanced around and said in a low voice, "One little slip like that could cost me my career."

"I'm sorry I forget whose company I'm in sometimes."

He cleared his throat and said, "I know you're a legend in Texas, but I didn't expect you to have a sense of humor."

It was CJ's turn to be embarrassed. "You must mean the event a few months ago. The press singled me out when it was really the Ranger SWAT team and about fifty other cops who did most of the work."

He shook his head, giving a non-verbal dismissal of her downplay of a recent event that made statewide news. "That's not what I was thinking about. I studied everything I could find about you taking out Bigalou Murphy and his biker buddy. I always wanted to ask why you turned down being a Texas Ranger."

"It's complicated," she replied in a soft voice. After a moment's silence, she looked him in the eye. "No, it's not that complicated. I turned it down because I believed the job offer was politically motivated. I still do. There are many more qualified women and men than me."

"I read somewhere that you said God told you not to take

the job."

"That's right, but many people either don't believe or understand, so I don't mention it unless I'm asked to explain, and I think it won't lead to a heated debate."

He looked away, as if searching for an elusive answer. "I'm not as young as I look, and I'm facing a crossroads. I could stay in for another eleven years, deploy to who-knows-where for who-knows-how-long, or I could make a career move before it's too late. You changed careers. Do you have any advice?"

"I get asked this question more often than you think by my officers. I've come up with a canned answer that I give everyone. It goes like this: Weigh, pray and stay."

His eyebrows rose to show he didn't understand.

"First, weigh your options. Make a list of all the pros and cons. Increase your knowledge and don't assume there's the perfect job waiting for you or the perfect place to live. The schools for your kids won't be perfect and your wife will have her own ideas on what you should do."

He nodded.

"Second, pray. I won't expound on that one other than to say take your time and don't underestimate the benefit of it."

"And third?" he asked.

"Stay until you're sure."

David caught her eye. The nudge of his head told her he was eager to leave.

The captain extended his hand. "I agree with everything you said, except one thing. You're more than qualified to be a Ranger."

She thanked him and joined David near the door.

"Talking business?" he asked.

"Uh-huh."

"Want to talk pleasure?"

"Let's do more than talk about it."

CHAPTER EIGHT

David stepped from the bathroom as the clock radio issued a rude buzz and the alarm on CJ's phone chirped at almost the same instant. Instead of her usual groping to quell the noise, she slid her legs from under the covers and was on her feet in a single motion.

"Good morning," said David. "Are you ready for coffee?"

"I'll get a shower first."

"Excellent choice. We have an early flight."

"Are you going to order breakfast?"

"Something light. It's only five-fifteen and we're getting a meal on the second plane."

CJ reached for the ceiling and wiggled her fingers. "You won a bunch of points for bringing me to the Hilton at the airport. I wasn't looking forward to a long drive this morning."

David moved to her. "It made more sense to leave yesterday and get a decent night's sleep. I knew you'd be talking with your mom until midnight if I didn't get you out of there."

CJ wrapped her arms around him. "I feel bad for not

spending more time with her." She looked up at him. "But not that bad."

"I'm glad she could come. I didn't want you worrying about Nancy and Davey being there alone."

She released him. "Me, worried? You're the one that didn't want them alone without a chaperone."

"Guilty as charged."

After sidestepping him, she spoke over her shoulder. "What time is our flight?"

"Boarding starts at eight fifteen."

"Where are we going?"

"Nice try. You'll find out when we check our bags."

The closed bathroom door and running water muffled her singing.

With a carafe of coffee and two continental breakfasts ordered, David dressed, smoothed the duvet, and placed the smaller of two suitcases onto the bed. With nothing to do but wait, he grabbed his phone. More out of habit than anything else, he checked his emails. Nothing of interest except Captain Crow's acknowledgment that he'd received the written report of the previous day's meeting, and he wanted David to attend the next meeting.

One thing David appreciated about his wife was her ability to shower, apply the modest amount of makeup she wore, dress, drink two cups of coffee, and be out the door in thirty-five minutes flat. Today, however, she took a little more time. Time off was beginning to work its magic on her.

David called the valet to bring their car around. It was waiting for them as he tossed the plastic room keys onto the front desk without slowing down. He could tell by CJ's long strides she was more than ready to leave troubles and cares behind, if for only a few days.

It took mere minutes before they parked and rolled suitcases into the terminal of Austin-Bergstrom Airport. Once inside, they waited in line to check their luggage. When it was their turn, David handed their passports to the ticket agent.

"Your destination?"

"Cozumel."

CJ's hand gripped his arm. "Perfect," she whispered.

The ticket agent handed him four boarding passes and a receipt for checked luggage. "You'll have a quick flight to Houston, where you'll change planes and go on to Cozumel."

They cleared security without a hitch. With plenty of time to kill before their flight, they burned off nervous energy by walking the length of the terminal. The call came for boarding, with priority given to those needing assistance, followed by first-class passengers.

"That's us," said David. "Row one, seats C and D."

CJ cocked her head. "You're earning more bonus points, Mr. Harper."

"I plan on redeeming them soon."

CJ sat by the window while David settled in the aisle seat. They held hands as a line of humanity passed by, some wearing suits and carrying briefcases and others sporting all manner of spring and summer apparel.

The line of people thinned to a trickle and ceased, as if someone had turned off a faucet. The flight attendant kept glancing at the open door and checking her watch. Then, the sound of a man's voice came from the other side of the bulk-head. "Hold your horses, we're coming."

Onto the plane came a man David judged to be about forty and a woman a few years his junior. The man's words came out loud and slurred. "I told you they wouldn't leave without us. That's why it pays to go first class."

"Not so loud," chided the woman.

CJ leaned into David. "It's a good thing this is a short flight. He must have started early this morning."

The flight attendant made a pass through the first-class section, securing the overhead bins. The man sitting across from David stopped her on her way back. "How 'bout you bring us a glass of bubbly?"

She smiled. "This is only a forty-five-minute flight and we don't want to be late getting to Houston. Fasten your seat belt and we'll be in the air in no time."

As the plane taxied, the man sitting across the aisle from David looked over at him. "Where ya' going, Bud?"

"Cozumel."

He turned to the redhead beside him. "Hear that, sugar? This guy and his girlfriend are going to Cozumel, too."

She responded with a pinched smile that showed her patience was wearing thin.

The plane rattled down the runway and climbed upward into a blue sky dotted with cotton-ball clouds.

The man spoke loud enough to turn heads. "It's a gyp, there's no champagne."

The plane reached cruising altitude and the smiling attendant came to take drink orders.

"Now I can have my champagne," said the man.

"I'm sorry, sir. I can only offer you coffee, a soft drink, juice, or water."

"No champagne? How are we supposed to start a honeymoon without champagne?"

"I heard you're going on to Cozumel. There'll be full service on your next flight."

The new bride said, "We'll each have a Sprite."

As the attendant worked her way down the aisle delivering drinks, the man took what looked to be a small bottle of mouthwash from his pocket and sloshed some contents into his glass of Sprite. He must have sensed David looking.

"A little trick a buddy of mine told me about. They don't check the small bottles of mouthwash in carry-on." He winked. "All you gotta do is empty the bottle and fill it with liquid courage. Want a snort?"

"A little early for me," said David.

After the plane landed, David told CJ not to let the wobbling man and his wife get away from them in the terminal. Once they cleared the jet bridge, David took the man by the arm. "Since we're both going to Cozumel, and we have time to kill, I thought we might get to know you and your wife. Have you ever visited the special lounge they have in this terminal?"

The man mumbled that he didn't know there was a special lounge.

"Your first-class ticket gives you access to it. There's a great view and all you can eat and drink." He led the man upstairs while CJ played along and made conversation with the woman. Soon, the couple sat in front of them in comfortable chairs.

Once the conversation reached a lull, David said, "Let me tell you a story about flying. I know this guy who planned a very special trip for his wife. He spent a lot of time making sure everything was perfect. Then, do you know what happened?"

Two heads moved side to side. "This drunk guy and his sweet wife got on the same airplane with my friend. The guy even brought his own liquor on the airplane with him, which is against all kinds of laws. Luckily, the flight attendant didn't see the bottle of booze. My friend thought the chances of the drunk being on the next flight were slim. But, as luck would have it, the drunk guy and his wife were booked on the next flight with my friend and his wife. Do you know what my friend did?"

Heads shook once more. "My friend found someone from the airline and told them about the guy bringing his own booze on the airplane and how drunk he was. The airline kept him from getting on the plane. He threw a fit and ended up getting arrested."

"That ain't right," said the man.

David tilted his head. "What's not right? The guy being drunk in public, breaking the law by carrying his own booze on board, or creating a disturbance?"

"All three," slurred the man. "It also wasn't right that your friend ratted on the guy."

CJ asked, "What else could my husband's friend have done?"

Both man and woman lifted their shoulders and let them drop.

CJ said, "I don't blame your friend. That would ruin a vacation for me. I think the guy should go to jail."

The eyes of the inebriate's wife widened in a plea for mercy. "Please tell me there's another way out for the guy who drank too much."

"There is," said David. "I told my buddy he didn't handle the situation right. All the wife had to do was get their tickets changed to a later flight. She could have kept him in the lounge and let the guy sober up. Look around, there's food and coffee and even places to take a nap."

The redhead stood and looked at CJ. "I need to powder my nose. Would you mind coming with me? I've only flown once in my life."

David turned so he could see the two women leave the lounge in a hurry.

In the meantime, the man turned pale. "Where's the bathroom? I'm not feelin' so good."

David walked the man to the bathroom and listened outside the stall as retching brought a quick end to the morning's party.

When the women returned twenty minutes later, the man was asleep on a couch.

"I don't know how to thank you," whispered the redhead. She looked away, seemed to collect her thoughts, and said, "He's never flown before and is scared to death. He hardly ever drinks and never the hard stuff."

"What was it?" asked CJ.

"Something my stepson brought back from spring break."

David and CJ exchanged glances.

"What happens if we miss our next flight?" asked the woman.

"You won't," said CJ. "Give him plenty of clear fluids after he wakes up. Try to get him to eat a little, but not too much. Sometimes that can make him sick again."

David added. "There's a shower he can use here in the lounge. That will help a lot."

The woman's eyebrows drew together. "Are you a cop or something?"

"State trooper, and CJ's an assistant chief of police. If your husband had boarded that next plane drunk, or carrying his own liquor, he'd be spending his honeymoon in either an American or Mexican jail."

They bid the grateful woman farewell and headed to their flight. The concourse looked as though someone had disturbed an ant bed as people scurried from one place to the next. CJ suggested another cup of coffee and a bathroom break, but not in that order.

As they approached their departure gate, David noticed a television monitor showing national news. The story didn't catch his eye, but a headline that crawled across the bottom of the screen did.

Two more Fort Hood soldiers dead from drug overdose. Secretary of Defense to testify.

"Did you see that?" asked CJ.

"Yeah."

She pulled his arm, and he followed her lead. They stood looking out at the airplane that would take them to tropical breezes and sandy beaches. "Are we finished with drugs and drunks for a while?"

"For five days."

She nestled next to him. "By the way. That was quite a story you told about your friend. You doubled your bonus points by getting them off the airplane."

"It was self-defense. We both need a break so we'll have clear heads when we get back. I have a feeling we're just getting started on something big."

CHAPTER NINE

The afternoon after they arrived back from vacation, David and CJ said hurried goodbyes to those assembled for the task force meeting and walked in sunshine to David's SUV. The meeting should have lasted an hour at the most, but had dragged on for three and a half. He could tell his wife wasn't hitting on all eight by her economy of words during the meeting and now, as they walked in silence across a parking lot.

After he had the engine running and the air conditioner blowing, CJ broke her silence. "We need to make a new family rule."

"What's this one?"

"Any time we go to a tropical island, we need a minimum of two more days off before we go back to work."

"A vacation to recover from the vacation? That's not a bad idea. It would have saved us from that meeting."

She turned to him. "I could barely keep my eyes open. That army captain is a nice guy and real smart, but his affinity with charts, graphs, and statistics had me pinching myself to stay awake."

"The amount of paper and words goes up with the size of the bureaucracy."

David faced her before he put the SUV in gear. "Is anything else bothering you? You don't seem yourself."

She took in a deep breath, puffed her cheeks, and let it out. "Sometimes I wonder if what we do makes any difference. Even if we catch whoever is selling moonshine and drugs, another low-level dealer will come in and take their place. We never get very far up the ladder. The real bad guys are so insulated by underlings and expensive lawyers, what do they have to fear? Even with the arrest of my crooked officer last December, we didn't get to the people who were running the organization."

"I thought you liked your job."

"I do." She paused. "Well, most of the time I do. Not so much today." She pointed to the road that would lead them to the interstate. "Let's get home. I need some time on the porch swing."

Normally the chatter on a police band radio didn't bother CJ, but today she must have tuned it out. A call for back-up from a highway patrolman both of them knew didn't get a rise out of her.

"Sounds like Smitty may have something interesting about twenty miles north of here," said David.

"Huh? Oh. Smitty. Right."

David stole a glance. "Are you still thinking about our vacation?"

She nodded. "I was remembering all the multi-colored fish." She placed a hand on his forearm. "Thank you for the vacation." Then, she reclined her seat and didn't speak again until she cleared her throat and put her phone on speaker. "What's up, Maria?"

"I wanted to follow up with you on a report of a missing student."

"Who is it?"

"A married grad student, Amy Sneller."

"Amy? How long has she been missing?"

"Since the day after you went to Cozumel."

"I didn't get through the stack of reports on my desk this morning. No one's heard from her?"

"Not a soul, but most of the people in her crowd wouldn't tell me if they did."

"Did you say Amy's married? I didn't have her pictured as having anything to do with men."

"That's what got me to thinking. Her husband hasn't called to check up on any progress we might have made."

CJ and David traded glances that told each other something wasn't right. "Where do they live?" asked David.

"On campus in the married students' apartments."

He looked with eyebrows raised in a non-verbal question. CJ nodded.

"David and I are coming into Riverview. Send me a text with the apartment number and we'll meet you there."

After she punched the red icon to disconnect the call, CJ looked wide awake.

"Who's Amy Sneller?"

"A clever grad student with an entrepreneurial spirit. Rumor has it she's the brains behind small-scale pot distribution to college students. From what we've been able to find out, she only allows non-felony sales to take place on campus and she never touches the product."

"Better the devil you know than the one you don't?" asked David.

"Something like that. John and I talked it over and concluded that with the trend toward decriminalization, we needed to focus on more important things."

David didn't disagree. "Tell me more about Amy."

"I'd describe her as a super-smart young woman who has

plans to go to a prestigious university in another state and pursue a doctorate. She's using her time here to save up a nest egg while she completes a master's degree."

It didn't take long before they arrived at the housing complex for married students. Maria met them on the sidewalk. "The husband's name is Lonny Martini. His car is here, so he should be."

The knock on the door brought an unshaven and disheveled man of about twenty-two years of age to the door. "Hi, Lonny, I thought I'd check back with you." Maria turned to CJ and David. "This is Assistant Chief Harper and her husband, David. Can we come in?"

His countenance took on the appearance of apprehension, but he scanned the room, nodded, and moved away from the door. The room had a spartan appearance with well-used furniture, a few prints on the wall, and dishes piled in the sink. Otherwise, the room had all the personal touches of a cheap hotel room.

David extended a hand and received an obligatory handshake. "Don't pay any attention to me. I'm just the chauffeur today. My wife and I had an out-of-town meeting, and we were going home when Maria called us."

CJ took over. "I wanted to tell you we take the disappearance of you wife seriously and we're doing everything we can to locate her. You haven't heard from her, have you?"

He shook his head but didn't invite them to sit.

"Did you and Amy have a falling out?"

His eyes broke contact. "No. We're cool."

"You don't have any idea where she might have gone?"

He raised his gaze from the floor. "She's a free spirit. The more I thought about it, she probably went to check out a doctoral program somewhere. It's not worth your time. She'll show up when she finds what she's looking for."

"Where?" asked CJ.

"Huh?"

"What university is she considering for her doctorate studies?"

"Oh." He paused a beat too long. "She said something about Stanford, or an Ivy League school, or even Oxford. Like I said, I don't think she's missing."

CJ nodded. "I'm sure you're right. That's probably where she went." She took a step toward the door. "We won't trouble you any more unless we hear something. Let us know if you hear from her so we can close out her file."

CJ turned to leave then stopped. "She took her cell phone with her, didn't she?"

"I guess so." He paused again for a second too long. "Now that you mention it, her phone was acting up. Wouldn't hold a charge. She's supposed to get a new one, but you know how broke grad students are."

CJ nodded in agreement. "It took me years to pay off student loans."

The three didn't speak until they huddled by David's SUV. He led off. "He's a terrible liar."

"About what?" asked Maria.

"Everything. To begin with, what was missing from the living room?"

CJ answered the question. "No wedding pictures. I bet if you look in any of these apartments you'll find framed photos of newlyweds."

David added. "Did you notice the door was open to one bedroom and nothing looked out of place? Lonny didn't impress me as a bed maker."

Maria slapped her forehead. "Lonny and Amy aren't married, are they?"

"I doubt it," said CJ. "That's the first thing on your list of things to do. Find out if they lied to save money on rent by claiming they're married."

CJ rubbed her chin. "What bothers me most is that he's not worried about her going missing. We need to find out why."

"He seemed worried the other day," said Maria. "I wonder what changed?"

"Something did. Do a thorough background check on Lonny. Everything you can find."

"Do you want me to tail him?"

"Not yet. Find out more about him first."

David chuckled as he started his SUV.

"What are you laughing at?"

"You."

"Me? Why?"

"A little earlier you were moaning about your job. Now you're like a bloodhound following a hot trail."

CJ took her time before answering. "Amy's too smart to draw attention to herself. Something's happened to her. I can feel it."

CHAPTER TEN

Instead of chancing what might be in the refrigerator, David suggested they grab a burger before calling it a day. The meeting with the task force seemed to be a waste of time, but it heartened him to see CJ come around when there was something to sink her teeth into. By the time he eased the SUV under the canopy of their carport, night shadows stretched long. He noticed Randy's car parked by the barn and the light from an open door spilled onto the pasture. Sandy, their shepherd mix, met CJ with a wagging tail.

After dispensing kind words and fingertip rubs from ears to ribs, CJ said. "We're going to the back porch. I need to think and Sandy needs a break from Nancy and Davey. He should be in bed by now, and I bet Nancy's at the table studying."

The trio walked together to the back porch until Sandy caught the scent of something on a southeast wind and trotted off to investigate. The porch swing squeaked a little as CJ perched on it. What didn't squeak was the back door when David turned the knob and gave it a push. The overhead lights in the breakfast nook shone down on the table covered with Nancy's computer and an array of papers, neatly stacked in piles for each subject.

He looked into the kitchen and checked the time on the microwave's clock. It was well past Davey's bedtime so he must be asleep. The only sign of him was a stuffed cat beside Nancy's backpack. He moved to the entrance of the living room, where silver shadows from the television danced across the living room furniture and walls. Otherwise, the room lay in darkness with the volume on the television barely audible.

Nancy's voice came from the side of the couch facing the television. "I said no, and I mean it. We can kiss, but that's all."

A deeper voice responded. "For now, but don't think I give up so easy."

David flipped the light switch and two yelps came from the hidden side of the couch. Then, a thud as a body hit the floor. Black hair came into view a split second before Randy rose to his feet. His eyes grew to dimensions better suited for a comic book.

"You!" shouted David.

Randy's hands went to shoulder height with palms facing out. "Please don't shoot me, Mr. David."

David looked down. His pistol was out of his holster and in his hand. Without breaking eye contact, he put it back where it belonged.

Nancy was already on her feet with her head down. The first plea came from her. "I'm so sorry, Mr. David. I'm so sorry."

He cut her off with a look he reserved for only the most egregious offenders he dealt with.

CJ and Sandy burst into the room. "What's going on?"

David couldn't speak.

"We were kissing," said Nancy in a mournful voice. "That's all. I promise."

David focused on Randy. "You two might have only been kissing tonight, but I've known plenty of guys like you. You have no respect for Nancy or our home."

Nancy sprinted toward her room, leaving Randy alone. David's mind filled with thoughts he believed were long gone. Now, the memories came back in amazing clarity. The previous year Randy was in high school, playing in a baseball game that would determine if he'd be awarded a college scholarship. The game didn't go his way, and he'd taken out his frustration by leading police on a high-speed chase through campus. CJ gave pursuit, ending in an accident that caused her to lose their first child. Everyone knew Randy was responsible, but his father lied, and he escaped punishment.

David may have been looking at Randy, but his vision was clouded with memories of CJ being loaded into an ambulance, followed by the scene of a small casket at graveside. Before he knew it, he had Randy by the back of his belt, marching him out of the house. "We gave you a second chance and a place to live. You're not getting a third."

CJ stepped in front of them. "David, stop."

He stepped around her with Randy's feet barely touching the ground. "Not this time."

Out the back door they went. With a single motion, he lifted and propelled Randy into the backyard where he landed in a heap. "Your father's in jail. That means the trailer you grew up in is empty. Get everything out of our fifth wheel, and I mean right now. If you come back on this property, what's left of you will go to jail."

He turned to see CJ with hands on her hips. "That wasn't necessary."

He tried to brush past her, but she grabbed his arm. "Go

for a walk, or a drive. Don't come back until you've calmed down." Her squinting eyes told him she wasn't in the mood for an argument.

The staring contest didn't last long. It was one thing to lay down the law to a teenager with over-active hormones and another thing to cross CJ when she squinted. He considered his options. "I'm going to see Dad and tell him he needs to find a new mechanic."

Tires spun and gravel flew as David sped away from their farm. After lowering herself onto the back porch swing, she folded her hands in prayer. "Lord, You know what happened here tonight, and that old wounds reopened. I ask that you bring comfort to Nancy. As for Randy and David, keep them safe until they calm down."

She looked out toward the river, intending on an extended time of prayer and silence. It wasn't to be. Randy started his car, spun gravel and drove it into the barn.

She didn't like the circumstances of David's speedy departure, but wouldn't go against his decision to evict Randy. It occurred to her a hasty decision had brought Randy to the barn in the first place, and another rash decision would take him away. The more she thought about it, the more she realized Randy never had to leave his home the night his father sliced his arm. Deputies had the elder McNutt in a patrol car by the time Nancy and Randy finished at the hospital.

CJ went back to alternating praying and thinking until Randy's car backed out of the barn and left in the same manner and direction as David. She looked at the dust he kicked up and shook her head. "What is it about men? They can't keep their foot off the accelerator when they're upset."

A few minutes later she heard the latch on the back door engage and Nancy spoke, "I heard him leave."

"He not only left, he left in a big hurry."

"Did you talk to him?"

"I've dealt with plenty of rowdy students and cantankerous men in life. Whenever possible, I let them calm down before I say anything to them."

Nancy settled on the swing with arms hugging herself. "I'm sorry Mr. David got so upset. I shouldn't have let Randy come in when you weren't home." Her head turned to look at the barn. "I'm glad he's gone. It saves me from telling him I don't want to be anything more than a friend."

"Is that how you normally tell boys you're not interested in them?"

The question came out harsher than CJ wanted it to, but Nancy came back with such a calm demeanor that it surprised her. "He started coming on to me as soon as you and Mr. David went on vacation. Me and your mom had a long talk about how I felt about Randy and how I could tell him I wasn't interested in him."

"What did my mother tell you to do?"

"She said a sharp knife cuts clean."

CJ couldn't help but chuckle. "That sounds just like her." She turned again to see Nancy's profile against the light coming from the barn. "Why didn't you take her advice?"

Nancy shrugged. "He asked to come in and watch television. I was studying when he said there was something interesting on the program he was watching." She shook her head. "Should have known better. The next thing I know, we're kissing. He's a much better kisser than I thought he'd be."

CJ covered a smile with her hand as Nancy kept talking. "I won't lie. I enjoyed it, but I wasn't about to go any farther. Anyway, that's about the time Mr. David came in and scared me out of at least three years of my life. I still can't believe he pulled out his pistol."

The swinging stopped. "He did what?"

"It must have been a reflex."

It was wrong, very wrong, for David to take out his pistol.

CJ determined to have a brief talk with him about it. She started the swing in motion again, this time a little faster. "We made a mistake allowing Randy to come live here on the property. He could have moved back home the night you took him for stitches."

Nancy's chin bobbed up and down. "I'm surprised Mr. David let him move into your travel trailer after what happened last year."

CJ looked into the night. "We're learning there's a difference between forgiving and forgetting. Sometimes the forgetting is harder."

"I don't want to forget my big mistake, even though I wouldn't trade Davey for the world."

Long seconds passed before Nancy spoke again. "On the way back from Padre Island, we girls had a discussion that has my head spinning."

"Oh?"

"It came from an ethics class one girl is taking. The professor asked if punishment and mercy can co-exist."

CJ had wrestled with that question in choosing a career in law enforcement, without much success. "What conclusions did you reach?"

"We didn't. Two said they couldn't, two said they could, and I said it depended on the severity of the offense and the circumstances."

"It seems there's a lot more to it than that."

"We found that out. Minds changed as we came up with unique examples. I don't think we solved anything, but the time passed in a hurry."

CJ's thoughts turned to Randy and how his recklessness cost her and David so much. Then, she thought of Holly Grimes and how the young woman's life ended so soon. Who was to blame? Holly? Whoever sold or gave her the alcohol and drugs? Society? Perhaps, nobody.

Nancy interrupted her musings when she rose from the swing. "I'd better get back to the books." She paused. "Do you think Mr. David will forgive me?"

CJ reached out her hand and Nancy took it. "I think he already has, but don't repeat what happened tonight."

"Don't worry about that. Any future dates are going to end this side of the door if you or Mr. David aren't home." She giggled. "That's assuming I'll ever have another date if word gets out about how he treated Randy."

"Do you know how that should make you feel?"

Nancy's red hair looked dark brown in the feeble light as she shook her head.

"Safe, Nancy. That's how you should feel."

BY THE TIME David reached his father's new digs, a lot of wind had gone out of his sails. The game of second guessing his actions was still in the first inning. Ninety-five percent sure he'd made the right decision to get Randy out of the trailer, he'd been heavy-handed in doing so. That left him with a large dose of guilt and the problem of how to tell his father Randy wasn't welcome on their property.

Bob opened the door and welcomed him in, saying nothing. He followed his father to the kitchen. Two glasses came from a cabinet over the dishwasher. "Iced tea or water?"

"Tea."

"Have a seat at the bar. I hear CJ gave you the boot."

"News travels fast in this town. Did she tell you why?"

"Nope. Just that you were coming, and you were nine shades of mad."

David remained silent until the tea arrived and he drained half of it. "I caught Randy and Nancy making out on the couch when we got home tonight. I threw him out.

Literally. He's gone and I don't want him back on the property."

His father nodded but said nothing for an uncomfortably long time. Finally, David asked, "No reaction or words of wisdom?"

Bob scratched his chin. "I remember your mother telling me about a sixteen-year-old boy she saw kissing his girlfriend in the den of our home. She said he looked a lot like you."

David shook his head. "That was different. Randy took advantage of us being gone. There's no telling what might have happened if we hadn't come home when we did."

His father smiled. "The only thing different between what happened twenty years ago and tonight is the year on the calendar and the people involved."

"Are you saying I shouldn't care what goes on in my home?"

"It's your property. You and CJ can run it however you want."

David lifted his gaze from a drop of condensation that ran down his glass. "That's one thing we agree on."

His father's hand covered the hand that wasn't clutching the glass. "There's more to this than two college freshmen kissing. You're still having trouble forgiving him for losing your daughter. I know because I still think about the people responsible for killing your mother. We can say we forgive them and mean it, but that doesn't mean the desire for justice or revenge gets any weaker."

After pulling back his hand, David stood and paced. "I thought I was over it and everything was all right between me and Randy. Then, when he told Nancy he wouldn't stop until he got what he wanted, I lost it."

He stopped pacing and looked at his father. "I scared myself, Dad. How I can ever look at Randy again and not see an image of our baby girl that never had a chance at life?"

"Some things take time. It hasn't been a year since you lost her."

He didn't try hiding the desperation in his voice. "What do I do in the meantime? I kicked him out and told him to move back into his father's trailer. I don't want him back."

"You don't have to do anything. He has clothes, food, a place to live, and a job at the university. He was getting along before you told him to move into your trailer." His father took another drink of tea. "Randy's been letting his studies slide. He's not interested in college and even if he passes this semester, he won't be going back in the fall."

That tidbit of information caught David off guard. "What about him working with you? I told him outright that he couldn't come back on the property. I didn't think about you when I said it."

Before he could say anything else, his father raised his hand. "Don't worry about that. I'm following your lead and building a shop before I start on my house. While you were in Cozumel, I contacted the same outfit that built your barn. The dirt work starts Monday. It's all metal, so it will be up by the end of the semester. I'm also having a water well dug. In the meantime, Randy can study and work as a janitor. It will be his choice to drop out of college or stay. After tonight, he might prefer to work as a mechanic in town. Dealerships and shops are always looking for skilled help. It won't hurt him to have some time to realize that his actions bring about consequences."

A movement outside caught David's eye. "Is someone out by the pool?"

"Alice is here. She had a rough day, so I cooked supper for her."

"I'm sorry I interrupted your evening."

His father waved off the apology and issued a mischievous

smile. "I'm glad CJ called before you showed up. You might have caught us making out."

David's mouth gaped open as his father burst into a boisterous laugh.

On the way home, it occurred to him his father might not have been kidding. You never knew with Bob Harper if he was pulling your leg or not.

CHAPTER ELEVEN

David yawned and drank coffee from a travel mug. The night had been short on sleep, even for him. CJ had been in the mood to talk after he made it home from his father's. She had to get a word-by-word playback of the conversation as they swung on the back porch. His voice and ears took a brief respite as he prepared for bed. Then CJ took her turn by recounting the conversation she had with Nancy. It surprised him neither CJ nor Nancy objected to Randy moving back to his father's trailer. That was the peaceful part of the conversation. CJ didn't hold back what she thought about him drawing his pistol.

She was right. It was a stupid thing to do.

On the way to Waco he monitored radio traffic. Something out of the ordinary was going on. A flurry of transmissions came from officers responding to a request for backup and a supervisor. It wasn't long before the transmission came from a voice that sounded calm and somber. "1523 to Bell County."

"Go ahead, 1523."

"10-79 to my 20 at Chalk Ridge Falls Park."

David knew the reason for the early morning buzz of radio traffic and the somber voice. Someone had died. The location of the body, near Stillhouse Hollow Dam, made him think the worst.

David looked at the caller ID after his cell phone came to life. It was a highway patrol officer both David and CJ knew well.

"John. What's up?"

"If CJ's still looking for a missing person, we might have found her. She fits the description, but there's no purse, phone, or car."

"In the park below the dam at Stillhouse?"

"Yeah."

"Does it look like a homicide?"

"More like an execution. Are you near enough that you can stop by?"

"I'll be there in fifteen minutes."

David waited until he told his phone to call CJ before he activated his emergency lights and pushed his vehicle up to ninety-five. She answered on the second ring, but he didn't give her a chance to speak. "Are you at work yet?"

"One block away."

"I need a photo of Amy Sneller."

"You sound like you're going somewhere fast."

"The park down from Stillhouse Dam. They found a body." He didn't need to tell her why he wanted the photo.

"You'll have it in five minutes."

Quick strides brought CJ into ACU's police department. Maria met her at the front door. All it took was one glance and Maria fell in behind her.

"Close the door."

Maria did as instructed and waited in silence until CJ sat behind her desk and opened a green file folder containing information on Amy. "David called. I don't have details yet other than there's a body near Stillhouse Lake in Bell County. They think it might be Amy."

CJ took out her phone and snapped two photos of Amy's picture ID. She attached them to a text and sent it.

"Do you want a cup of coffee before I tell you what I found out about Amy?" asked Maria.

CJ looked up at Maria. As usual, she'd dressed down to look more like a student than a cop. She wore a windbreaker over a plain blouse, skinny jeans, and black shoes that looked like a cross between hiking boots and tennis shoes. "No. I had plenty at home, and it may be a busy morning if it's Amy. I don't want to get too wired."

Maria pointed to the folder. "I put my written reports in the file, but I'll give you the short version. Amy and Lonny Martini aren't married, unless they slipped off to Mexico or some other country."

"I doubt she'd do that."

"She has no recent credit card activity for airline tickets or anything related to travel, but her car isn't on campus. We checked everywhere."

CJ nodded. "That's at least one strike against Mr. Martini for lying to us."

"Do you want me to pick him up?"

She leaned back in her chair and flipped through a page in the file. "Not yet. David will call as soon as he knows for sure if it's Amy." She tapped the photo. "I remember Amy having tattoos starting at her neck and running down her arm all the way to her wrist."

CJ picked up her phone. "If there's anyone who's an expert on ink, it's our favorite pastry chef, Yari."

After the usual salutations and receiving an invitation to

come dip fresh biscotti in Honduran coffee, CJ got down to business. "I'm sitting here with Maria. We got to talking about tattoos and I was trying to remember what Amy Sneller's looks like. I know she has them all down her right arm, but I can't remember what any of them are."

Yari's laugh always seemed to bubble out of her like fizzy water. "Most of them have something to do with pot. There're plants, pipes, bongs, and streams of smoke. The one with the best color is a field in Hawaii. It's on her back. She gave me a private viewing last year before I reformed."

"Thanks. I may not make it in today, but I'll try to come by tomorrow."

Once again, CJ placed a call to David.

"I'm almost there," he said before she could speak.

"Look for tattoos running down her right arm. Most have something to do with pot. There's a mural on her back of a field of weed in Hawaii."

"That's pretty specific. How did you find out so quick?"

"I called Yari."

"Should have known. Thanks."

With her phone back on her desk, CJ pulled a yellow legal pad in front of her. "I'd better start a list of names and times of people I speak to today. If it turns out to be Amy, we'll need a search warrant for her and Lonny's apartment." She looked at Maria perched on the edge of a chair, looking like she couldn't wait to be doing something besides sitting and waiting on a phone call.

"Do you know Lonny's class schedule?"

Maria was on her feet before the end of the sentence. "I'll get it."

She returned in time to hear David's call come in. CJ took in a deep breath before she answered. "Yeah?"

"It's Amy," he said, in a sure, subdued voice.

"I was afraid you'd say that."

"I'm glad you called with the description of the ink on her arm and back."

"Are you going to stay there long?"

"Bell County detectives are on their way. I'll tell them what I know and ask them to call you. This is their turf, so it will be up to the sheriff to decide how he wants to proceed with the investigation."

CJ knew about jurisdictional lines and how some departments worked well with others, while others didn't. Sometimes it came down to personality clashes between the investigators, or political considerations. She chose her words with care. "Tell them I can get search warrants and serve them to save time."

David's voice came in a whisper. "Why don't I tell them the truth? Maria's sitting on pins and needles, ready to sink her teeth into a murder investigation."

CJ ignored the comment and asked, "Are you going on to Waco?"

"I called Captain Crow and let him know where I was and what I'm doing. He told me to come to his office after I spoke with the detectives." He paused. "They just drove up. I'll see you tonight."

Maria sat with arms crossed. "I know we don't have the lead, but Amy was one of ours. Are you sure we have to wait? Isn't there something else we can do?"

After drumming her fingertips on the desk, CJ asked, "Do you have your red wig handy?"

Maria rose from the chair. "It's in the trunk of my car, along with my over-sized sunglasses."

"Find Lonny Martini and trail him the rest of the day or until you hear otherwise from me or the chief."

Maria's footfalls peppered the hallway as CJ flipped a page on the legal pad and wrote her next steps. She knew the list would grow as the day wore on.

The first call went to John, her boss. The voice of a pre-teen girl answered.

"Is this Hope or Faith?"

"Hope. I guess you need to talk to Daddy."

"He can call me back if he's busy."

The next voice came from John. "Sorry about that. Both girls think it's their responsibility to answer any phone that rings, including my cell."

The conversation didn't take long since details were in short supply. After giving the bare-bone facts, CJ asked, "Do you want me to call Alice?"

"Go ahead. I'm on my way. Perhaps you'll hear from the Bell County detectives by the time I get there."

The phone call to Alice brought the same response as when Holly died, genuine grief over the loss of another young life. After hanging up, CJ thought of how multidimensional the university president was. Underlying all the skills was a genuine love for the students. To lose one to an accident, suicide, or other unforeseen event always took its toll on her.

CJ's musings took an unexpected turn when she considered that Alice might someday be David's stepmother. Where that thought came from she didn't know, but she didn't have long to consider it as her cell phone jangled.

"Hello?"

"Assistant Chief Harper? This is Detective Holloway with Bell County SO. Your husband told me you could get a search warrant for Amy Sneller's apartment."

"We'll be glad to assist in any way we can."

"That's music to my ears. We're down two detectives and stretched thin."

"Text me your e-mail address and I'll send you everything we've gathered so far. Did David give you any background on Amy?"

"He said you'd be the best source for that."

"This won't be in the documents you'll receive, but she was a small-time marijuana dealer here in Riverview. She was smart enough to insulate herself with a delivery team."

The sound of a quick exhalation of breath came from the phone. "That's not good news. We're getting reports that dealers in the area are being pressured to expand their product line to include the hard stuff, including fentanyl."

A shiver went down her spine. "I remember something about that from the last task force meeting."

With a promise to keep Detective Holloway informed, it was time to get to work. As soon as she had the search warrant in hand, she and Maria could pay a visit to Lonny Martini. The first arrest in the case might be only a few hours away.

CHAPTER TWELVE

By the time the judge reviewed the request for a search warrant, the courthouse bell tolled four times. The sound competed with rumbles of thunder and the onset of a heavy spring rain. CJ sprinted to her car and beat the worst of the torrent by mere seconds. Before she started the university patrol car, she dredged her phone out of her purse. David answered with the sound of highway noise in the background. "I hope you're calling with good news."

"Not yet. How about you?"

"Killeen PD found Amy's car in the lot of a hotel, parked in a spot where security cameras couldn't see it. There's no telling how long it sat there before being noticed. The guys in white plastic suits are going over it."

Rain pounded her car with such ferocity she had to press the phone firm against her ear and speak up. "Did Amy check into the hotel?"

"If she did, she used a fake ID. Detectives are reviewing several days of video to make sure, but I think it's a waste of time. I'm leaning more toward her meeting someone and going with them."

"It could have been her supplier."

A crack of thunder came before David could respond.

"Holy guacamole," said CJ. "That was close."

"The line of storms must be where you are. I've been in rain for the last twenty minutes."

"How close are you?"

"Five miles out of Riverview."

"Judge Kemp stayed tied up in court for most of the afternoon. I finally got him to sign a search warrant for Amy's apartment. Do you want to meet me there?"

"Sure. What about Lonny?"

CJ started the car. "Maria's been shadowing him all day wearing her red wig. You'll enjoy hearing what she observed him doing today."

"That's good; I need something to cheer me up. I've been reading reports of arrests for bootleg moonshine and EMS reports of fentanyl OD's. The latest was a middle school student in Belton. Guess what they found."

She thought for a few seconds before the answer came to her. "A lollipop laced with fentanyl."

"Brains and beauty. I'm a very lucky man."

"Yes, you are." She disconnected the call, smiled, and backed away from the curb.

***

THE RAIN HAD MOSTLY STOPPED by the time David pulled his car into an empty spot in front of the two-story apartment complex at the northwestern edge of Agape Christian University. From prior conversations with CJ and his recent visit, he knew most of the residents of these spartan, putty-colored apartments were nearing the end of their college days. The cars dotting the parking lot were a rogue's gallery of dents, fading paint, and mismatched tires. Some still had the look of money, but taken as an aggregate, they spoke of men and women deferring gratification by buckling down with their studies and getting educations.

Maria and CJ met him on the sidewalk leading to Amy and Lonny's apartment, a ground floor unit without identification or decoration except for the number 113 in bold numbers on the wall facing the street. Not the luckiest of numbers he mused to himself.

CJ's knock preceded a face glimpsing through parted mini-blinds, followed by the click of a lock and a dead bolt. The door opened and Lonny took several steps back from the door of an apartment that smelled of trash left too long before being taken out. The skin around his eyes had the look of old pottery glaze that had crackled into a random mosaic of lines. His countenance spoke of worry mixed with fear.

In a voice that blended authority with compassion, CJ said, "Lonny, we need to talk to you about Amy."

"I already know," he said.

"How?" asked David.

Lonny looked down. "It doesn't matter."

David and CJ traded glances. She cast her gaze again to the young man. "I have search warrants for your apartment and car. Do you want to read them?"

He shook his head.

"You need to tell us, Lonny."

"No. I don't want to read them," he whispered.

"I need the keys to your car," said CJ.

From a belt loop of dirty jeans, he unclipped a chain. He pulled the chain and a set of keys slid from his pocket as if it was a fish on a metal line.

Maria held out her hand for the keys. "I'll search his car. I watched him today and I think I know where to look. Do you want me to call any additional officers?"

CJ spoke as she moved to the kitchen. "I'll do it."

Lonny sank onto a threadbare couch, his gaze on the floor.

David rolled a secretarial chair from the desk against the far wall and pushed it to a spot close to Lonny. He settled in and stared at the young man with wispy sideburns and a mustache that looked like a stain from chocolate milk. "What did you hear about Amy?"

"Nothing."

"You said you did."

"I have nothing to say."

David knew he had to tread lightly. "You're right, but we haven't advised you of your rights. Right now, we're just two guys talking." It was a peremptory strike. If Lonny demanded a lawyer, they'd get nothing of value from him.

CJ joined them, carrying a baggie containing what looked to be dried, ready-to-roll marijuana in it. "Did you mean to leave this on the kitchen counter in plain sight?"

David put on a pair of latex gloves, took the baggie, opened it, sniffed, and resealed it. His stare at the young man intensified. Instead of threats of punishments, he took a more circuitous approach to getting information by saying, "Look at me."

The head came up as if cranked slowly until cloudy eyes gazed into his.

"I've seen plenty of scared people in my life and you're right there at the top. We all know you left that pot out so we would find it. That tells us you wanted to get caught."

CJ sat beside Lonny. "Is that what you want? Do you want us to bust you so you'll be somewhere safer?"

He nodded.

CJ recited the standard warning and said, "As of now, you're not under arrest, but you are being detained."

David knew Lonny would either clam up and demand an attorney, or he'd talk. He needed one more push. After relaxing in the chair and acting as if he didn't care, he said, "One thing you need to consider. We don't have to arrest you. In fact, that might be the best thing to do. Of course, the word might get out that you avoided going to jail by giving us information. With Amy already lying in the morgue that might not be the best decision you could make."

CJ spoke in her most sympathetic voice. "I know you want the people punished who killed Amy."

The pinched eyebrows spoke without words. The young man, caught in a vice of two evils, had a decision to make. Which way would he decide?

His posture stiffened. "I'm not saying anything else without a lawyer."

"Have it your way," said David.

CJ told him to stand up and turn around. The detainment morphed into an arrest. He made a weak verbal reply that he understood. Another officer arrived and CJ told him to take Lonny to the interview room at the university police department.

David and CJ started in the bedrooms, working methodically to search for anything drug related or that might help in the murder investigation. He heard CJ call for cardboard boxes. An array of items including laptops, thumb drives, notebooks, a diary and an assortment of seemingly random things found their way into the cache of items. A question came to David's mind. He stepped to the neater of the two bedrooms where his wife was elbow deep in a file cabinet. "Are you and Maria going to process everything that's being tagged?"

She looked up. "We're only conducting the search and starting the chain of custody. Bell County detectives will send someone to pick this up either tonight or in the morning."

He nodded. "That's what I thought, but I wanted to make sure." After looking around he asked, "Anything interesting?"

"Not in here. Her laptop or diary may hold hidden secrets, but I've seen nothing of value yet. What about you?"

"Dirty clothes and dirty magazines. Otherwise, nothing. I think he brought the baggie in with him from his car so we'd find it."

CJ pushed the drawer of the file cabinet closed. "What's your gut telling you?"

"Lonny's a lot more afraid of who killed Amy than he is of us." He paused. "You said something when I was on the road about Maria observing something I might be interested in. What was it?"

"I had her follow Lonny today. After he got out of class, he went to a convenience store off the interstate. A car pulled up alongside his and they made an exchange of some sort."

"Did she get photos?"

"She took photos with her phone. She didn't get close, but they can be enhanced."

"Did she get the plates of the vehicle the delivery guy was driving?"

"The angle's bad, but at least it's a partial."

For the first time since Holly Grimes died, they had a concrete lead. It might not connect with Amy's murder, but then again, drugs and homicide have a habit of running in pairs. "Anything else?"

"Lonny made several stops around town with college students, but never on campus."

"Did Maria take photos of those too?"

"And video. We already have names of the buyers. Our bloodhound did an outstanding job."

David wondered out loud. "Lonny wanted us to catch him and put him in jail. He knew he'd only get a ticket for simple possession of a baggie of weed. He even left it in plain sight on the kitchen counter. What if he knew Maria had him under surveillance?"

"Then he knew we'd arrest him for dealing if we found enough evidence."

David scratched his chin. "This makes no sense. Even for dealing small amounts of weed, the courts won't throw the book at him."

The front door to the apartment opened and then shut. Maria entered the bedroom carrying two brown paper bags. Without speaking, she dumped the contents of the first bag on Amy's bedspread. Out fell another baggie of marijuana.

"What's in the other bag?" asked CJ.

Maria remained mute, but a sparkle in her eyes spoke of discovered treasure. She moved to a separate section of the bedspread and upended the sack with the flair of a magician. Out fell a dozen lollipops, each neatly wrapped.

"Holy smoke," said CJ. "If that's what I think it is, you hit the jackpot."

David's thoughts went into overdrive.

CJ asked, "Anything else in his car?"

Maria ended her silence. "Five cases of plastic water bottles in the trunk. I wondered why Lonny and the person who delivered to him both backed into the parking spaces at the side of the store."

The tumblers in David's brain all fell into place at the same time. "Now I see what's going on. Someone in Killeen wanted to expand. Amy didn't. The easiest way to develop a new territory is to take over an existing delivery network. In the business world, it's called mergers and acquisitions. There was no room for a headstrong woman like Amy who didn't want to expand."

His wife's gaze locked on the lollipops. "Bag and tag. Call for a wrecker. I want that car torn apart from bumper to bumper. Get a sniffer K9 to help you."

In a matter of seconds, David was once again alone with his wife. They looked at each other, both knowing the ramifications of the discovery of all three substances together. Someone was expanding their drug business into Riverview. Lives had already ended and there would probably be more. "I need to call Captain Crow and let him know what we found."

CJ nodded. "I'll call John and the deputy from Bell County."

After gathering the lollipops, David added his name to the chain of custody slip Maria had attached to the bag. "I'll get these to the State lab. I don't want us to mention the video to the Bell County detectives until I've tracked down the delivery car and find out who the driver is."

David moved closer to her and looked into brown eyes that communicated deep concern. He didn't sugarcoat his words as he pointed down to the bag of lollipops. "If these turn out to be laced with fentanyl, Lonny's facing a long prison sentence. That means he's more afraid of whoever is behind this than he is of years in a Texas prison and we're dealing with some bad people."

Her chin dipped and rose three times. "Terrible people." She seemed lost in thought and then said, "I wasn't expecting moonshine to be part of the bargain."

He shrugged. "One-stop shopping. Give the customers anything they want. It won't surprise me if you find a stash of other drugs in Lonny's car."

Reaching down, David picked up the bag of lollipops. "You and Maria finish up here. Captain Crow will want to know if they laced these lollipops with fentanyl ASAP."

"A field test won't be enough?"

"Not this time. I don't want some hot-shot defense attorney putting doubts in jurors' minds about the validity of the tests. There's too much at stake with this case to make any mistakes."

CJ looked around the room. "You might be home before

me. I need to finish searching, formally charge Lonny, take him to county jail, and then get the detectives from Bell County to come pick up the evidence we collected and write a detailed report."

David paused before leaving. "What's your next step tomorrow?"

After straightening her posture, CJ blinked three times. "Let's see. Maria and I will work on tracking down all the students who took delivery of something Lonny was selling. It will probably be a full day of research and possibly some interviews."

David came to her, and she moved into his open arms. He gave her a long hug, feeling the tension in her back relax just a little. "Let's not forget to save a little time for us."

She pulled back and winked. "Let's both try to get home before midnight."

CHAPTER THIRTEEN

Dark circles under her eyes marked the telltale signs that CJ had a late night and started her day too early. To make things worse, little Davey didn't hesitate to let the world know how it displeased him to have another tooth cut through his lower gum. Even Nancy seemed uncharacteristically out of sorts. A midnight farm emergency of a sheep struggling to give birth to twins turned into a multi-hour ordeal with her and her vet employer saving one lamb and losing the second. She hated to lose an animal and spent an exorbitant number of words rehashing what they could have done to change the outcome.

CJ escaped her home as soon as possible. Maria's car sat parked in front of the ACU police department when she arrived, which was not uncommon for her eager-beaver detective. What surprised her was to see John Sylvester's vehicle parked in the spot reserved for the chief of police at this early hour. Maria's accented words filtered out of John's office and into the hall. Instead of joining them right away, CJ retrieved her third cup of coffee for the day and grimaced as she tasted the brew that reminded her of a cross between scorched grinds and hot roofing tar. "Lieutenant Grimes must have made the coffee again."

Maria sat drinking a Red Bull, looking bright-eyed and ready to conquer the world. "That coffee is nasty."

"Not much sleep at the Harper's home last night. Nancy was out late on a farm call, I had to pick up Davey from Aunt Bea's at midnight, and he's cutting teeth. David got tied up on the way back from Austin with a trooper calling for help at a traffic stop. He literally fell into bed about three thirty. If it wasn't for this coffee, you'd be looking at my eyelids."

John formed his forefingers into the semblance of a church steeple and tapped his lips. "I've given this thought and we need to re-prioritize our duties. CJ, I want you and Maria to devote most of your time to investigating and putting an end to the drugs and alcohol on campus. I realize we can never eliminate them all, but we can't lose another student to overdose or jail. We advertise ourselves as a Christian university where people come to get a top-notch education, without most of the distractions of secular universities. I know it sounds like a cliché, but our reputation is at stake, not to mention the school's finances."

"Won't that stretch you too thin?" asked CJ. "After all, you're hired to spend half your time teaching."

"I'll still do the lectures, but I have a grad student who can handle my office hours, grading exams and other duties. We'll need to run it by Alice, but I'm sure she'll agree when we tell her what you two found last night." He handed sheets of paper across the desk that outlined existing and proposed duties.

"When will you present this?"

"You and I are to be in her office at nine."

"Not Maria?"

He shook his head.

"Thank goodness," said Maria. "President Cummings

scares me. It's like she can take one look and know what I'm thinking."

CJ grinned, but soon the seriousness of the tasks ahead brought the corners of her mouth down. She cast her gaze to John. "Maria and I will review the photos and video she took yesterday, identifying the students who bought from Lonny and putting together a file on each one until we have full backgrounds. I want to identify the weakest ones and get them in first for questioning. We'll work our way through them until we've interviewed them all. A firm threat of getting kicked out of school might make them think twice."

John nodded an affirmation. "That reminds me. I haven't had time to read all the reports. Did you find anything else in Lonny's car?"

CJ motioned for Maria to answer. "There was a false bottom in the center console. I missed it, but the K9 didn't. We found small quantities of powdered cocaine, amphetamines, crack cocaine and some black tar heroin."

John groaned.

CJ ran a finger around the rim of her mug. "David made the comment yesterday that it looked like one-stop shopping for almost anything illegal."

John shook his head. CJ wasn't sure if it was a sign of disgust or deep concern. "Everything from booze and pot to stuff that will stop a heart. Mobile drug stores for middle school children up to senior citizens."

Being focused on the campus, CJ had thought little about the bigger picture. Words spilled out before she thought them through. "That may be a weak point for whoever is behind this. They may try to do too much."

John tracked what she was saying. "That's good. It goes along with your idea of finding the weak links and getting them to talk."

"Anything else?" asked CJ.

"I have an eight o'clock class. I'll meet you at Alice's office at nine."

Maria was on her feet and the first out the door.

CJ shook her head and smiled. "She can say what she wants about my drinking coffee, but those energy drinks get her wound up tight."

Maria had the video feed on a monitor ready to play when CJ entered her office. The next hour sped by as they viewed still images and videos of people making purchases of products ranging from a clear liquid in plastic bottles to things so small they transferred from one palm to the next without coming into view. Not all the buyers were students, which added another layer of law enforcement agencies and departments to the list of those to be notified. But not right away. Not until she'd interviewed the students Maria caught on film.

With her mind fully engaged on what she'd seen, CJ walked across campus to the administration building, a multi-storied stone building with white columns guarding the entrance at the top of slate steps. She looked up to the top floor and the windows of the office on her far left. Behind those windows waited Alice Cummings, President of Agape Christian University and girlfriend of her father-in-law. How strange that last title sounded when applied to a university president, like something reserved for a teenage romance.

CJ paused in thought before climbing the steps. What was the word Alice used to describe their relationship? "A *silventure,*" she whispered. It was obvious she'd spent some time thinking about it when she explained she had borrowed syllables from three words: *sil* from silver to indicate age, *ven* from venerate, to show esteem, and *ture* from adventure. A new adventure for seasoned people with someone they held in high regard. Leave it to Alice to make up a word where none existed. If Alice spent that much time coming up with a word to describe her and Bob's relationship, it must be getting serious.

CJ couldn't help but smile as she bounded up the steps. There could be worse things than having Alice for a mother-in-law.

After being waved in by Alice's gatekeeper and personal assistant, CJ settled in a chair beside John in front of her desk. Alice joined them and made a triangle with a third chair. Her silver hair looked as it always did, shimmering in the light with a glow of platinum, and not a lock out of place. She crossed her legs at the ankles and sat with a posture that communicated confident sophistication, yet approach-ableness.

"This must be important," said Alice as a way of beginning the conversation.

John nodded. "I may go over some things you're already aware of, but I think it's good you hear the complete story, up to this point." He started with the death of Holly Grimes then gave an update on the murder of Amy Sneller.

Alice stopped him with an upraised hand. "Are you saying the two deaths are linked?"

John looked at CJ, her clue to join the conversation. "We've been aware of Amy being the leader of a small mari-juana delivery group for some time. From what we've learned over the last couple of years, she sold nothing herself. She seemed to have a policy that her underlings always sold in small quantities. That way the end user would only get a ticket if caught."

She knew the next words would be unwelcome, but neces-sary. "We're working on the theory that Amy's murder results from her being unwilling to sell much harder drugs. Last night we arrested Lonny Martini, Amy's roommate here in the married couple's housing. They never legally married, but that doesn't matter now. Lonny received a shipment yesterday of several cases of moonshine, marijuana, and all kinds of illegal drugs to sell, including fentanyl."

"Was the delivery on campus?"

John took over. "Not the delivery. We obtained search warrants for his car and apartment. Only a baggie of pot was found in their apartment, but his car was another story."

CJ leaned forward. "If there's a silver lining to this dark cloud, it's that Detective Vasquez trailed Lonny from the time he finished his last class until he arrived back at his apartment several hours later. She took photos and videos of him receiving the stockpile of drugs and moonshine and making deliveries to people in town. Most of the purchases were by our students."

It always amazed her that Alice could keep a poker face in almost any situation. Years of dealing with politicians, irate parents, recalcitrant students, and finicky professors had steeled her nerves to the point she maintained a professional decorum when most people would fly off the handle.

Alice folded her hands in her lap. "I thought we'd get a reprieve after you rid our community of the last drug dealers. I should have known better."

"We may have created a void that was waiting to be filled," said CJ. "Most of the activity seems to be concentrated in Bell County, around Fort Hood and Killeen. I think Riverview County and ACU are afterthoughts. Amy had a small organization the big dealer could test the waters with. David called it mergers and acquisitions."

John's head nodded. "We might be in better shape than other communities, but I don't want to take any chances."

Alice's eyebrows raised with interest. "What do you propose?"

John handed Alice copies of the same pages he'd given to Maria and CJ earlier. "I want to relieve CJ of some of her administrative duties so she and Maria can devote themselves full time to making sure hard drugs don't take hold here. I'd like to implement this at least until the end of the semester."

Alice took her time studying the pages. She could digest written information with speed and make firm, well-reasoned decisions. She nodded. "Implement these changes immediately. The way the regents are breathing down my neck, I can ill afford any sort of scandal." She looked at CJ and then John with a hint of fatigue. "I don't suppose you know of any way to minimize the publicity of Amy's death and the arrest of Lonny Martini."

John answered first. "Bell County is investigating Amy's murder. As tragic as it is, it didn't occur anywhere near here, so the only link to the university is that Amy was our student. We have no actual proof she was involved in any sort of drug activity, so we should be in the clear for the immediate future. That may change if the killers ever stand trial."

"As for Lonny," said CJ, "all we found in his apartment was a small bag of marijuana. All the serious drugs, including fentanyl, were in his car, which we hauled off campus last night. Also, he and Amy never married, so I don't think a nosy reporter will dig deep enough to put together Amy's death and Lonny's arrest."

"What about the students you observed buying drugs yesterday?"

John nodded for CJ to respond. "As of now, only five of us know about the people who bought drugs or alcohol from Lonny yesterday: John, Maria, me, David and you. David has the video Maria took of Lonny receiving the shipment. He's trying to identify the seller before he shares the video with detectives from Bell County. As far as they're concerned, they came here last night to pick up items related to Amy's murder. They might find something related to her pot business on her computer, but I doubt it. She may have gotten herself killed, but she impressed me as shrewd in running her illegal business."

"Time," said Alice with a wistful stare. "I need to get through this semester and into summer without a scandal. If I can do that—"

She left the rest of the sentence unsaid and stood. "I appreciate everything you've done and continue to do. Keep me posted on any developments."

John and CJ walked down the steps of the administration building without talking. He broke the solitude of her thoughts where the sidewalk divided. "Are you coming back to the office now?"

"I need coffee that won't take the varnish off my desk if I spill it. I'll be there in a few minutes."

Even though he was several inches shorter than she was, John's love of running marathons meant he was used to taking off at a good clip. It didn't take long for him to round a corner and be out of sight. She needed to amble and think. The morning was right for it, with spring sunshine warming her and the campus foliage in full bloom.

What was so special about Alice making it until summer? Was her job in imminent jeopardy? What about her relationship with David's father? Would the regents force her to choose between a relationship and her job?

As if on auto-pilot, she opened the door to the Student Union, home of the Campus Grind along with other offices and shops. Before entering, she gazed through the plate glass windows to see if Aunt Bea was holding court. She wasn't, but another familiar face caught her eye. Randy sat in a booth, leaned forward, listening intently to the same preppy-looking young guy she'd seen having a tense conversation with Amy several weeks ago. Instead of going in, she worked her way to a back loading dock and entered the bistro through a delivery entrance.

Yari looked up from decorating a tray of pastry with a piping bag. "You lost?"

CJ motioned Yari to join her. They moved to a swinging door with a window in it, which gave them a limited view of tables, including the one Randy and the young man occupied. CJ asked, "That guy with Randy. Isn't his name Peter Starks?"

Yari nodded a head of purple hair. "That's him. He's in here almost every day. Reminds me of a vulture, or a salesman. I put those two in the same category. He's always looking around like he wants to sell life insurance or something."

"What else do you know about him?"

"He wears a Rolex and dresses like he's going to a photo shoot."

"Anything else?"

"Not really," she paused. "Except he talks to all kinds of people." She pointed with an extended index finger. "Take Randy, for example. Look at them and tell me what those two could have in common."

Yari was right. Blue jeans, T-shirts, and Walmart tennis shoes for Randy, while Peter wore designer apparel from his button-down shirt to his leather loafers without socks.

"Do you want me to introduce you?"

CJ answered with a shake of her head then reached in her pocket and pulled out a debit card. "Would you mind getting me my usual? I'm too busy to be socializing today."

"How about a bear claw? They're still warm."

She continued to stare at the two young men. "No thanks. I gained a little weight on vacation and it seems to be intent on staying." She stood back and allowed Yari to retrieve her coffee. She made a mental note to do a background check on a handsome young man wearing a gold Rolex on his left wrist. A talk with Randy might also be a good idea.

CHAPTER FOURTEEN

Thoughts of interviews with students faded as CJ turned off the farm-to-market road and her SUV skipped across the cattle guard. The repurposed railroad tracks served as the dividing line between their property and the rest of the world. Tension from the denials and lies she'd heard that afternoon melted away like ice on sunbaked asphalt as she took in the view of cattle munching green blades of grass and a calf with its head at an angle, nursing. She glanced at the clock on the dashboard and realized she had time to weed the small garden she planted. Putting on jeans and boots would be a welcome relief after a day in slacks and a blazer.

Her eyebrows rose as she turned the corner and saw David's work SUV. She remembered him saying he planned to work from home unless Captain Crow needed him elsewhere. As she swung her vehicle under the carport, she noticed her husband wearing a bathing suit and cleaning the pool.

She grabbed her purse and walked across grass that had a healthy spring to it. "It must be nice to loaf around all day."

He kept his head down and pushed a long-handled brush

down the pool's side. "I told you I was working from home today."

"All day?" she asked.

His head jerked up, and his voice held an edge. "You sound like Captain Crow. Yes. All day."

She hooked her hands on her hips and stared. "What's wrong?"

"Nothing worth mentioning." His gaze went back to the task at hand.

She knew she should walk away and say nothing. She complied with half of the internal warning, but the words were past her lips before she could cram them back down. Speaking over her shoulder as she walked, she said, "You're not the only one who had a long day. Plan on fixing your own supper tonight."

David's laugh followed her into the house.

"What's Mr. David laughing about?" asked Nancy after the door closed too firmly.

CJ looked down at the skinny teen with red hair going in directions that defied gravity. Before her, as usual, lay a scattering of books and a laptop. Little Davey scrambled in his playpen and extended pudgy hands. She lifted the lad and settled him on her hip as she answered Nancy's question. "That husband of mine is growling tonight. Better steer clear. I made the mistake of asking him what was wrong."

"Um. And what did you say when he snarled?"

"I told him he wasn't the only one who had a bad day and he could fix his own supper."

Luckily Nancy's hand paused on the way to her mouth with some of Davey's Goldfish crackers, or there would have been orange chunks sprayed on her computer. She looked up. "He always cooks. Your idea of an oven timer is the smoke alarm."

CJ bristled. "Even if that's true, it's not a nice thing to say."

Nancy shrugged and turned back to her computer.

It was then CJ noticed the warmth of Davey against her hip and the coy look on his face. She placed him back in the playpen and observed a wet circle on her slacks. "When was the last time you changed his diaper?"

"Uh..."

"That's what I thought."

Nancy stood and went to work stripping off her son's clothes. Her words came out terse and defensive. "You two aren't the only ones with problems. I was so worn out from my late night I made an eighty-nine on a test today."

"That's not bad," said CJ.

Nancy bolted upright. "Not bad? It's a B. I don't make B's —ever. My scholarships depend on me making straight A's. How am I supposed to do that raising a baby and staying up all night on stupid farm calls?"

The sound of a splash found its way to the breakfast nook. All CJ could see of David was his head and toes as he floated in the pool. She turned back to Nancy. "Don't put a diaper on him."

"Why not?"

She lifted the squirming boy and carried him outside. Once she reached the side of the pool, she hollered at David. She extended her arms and gave him a bare-bottomed baby. "It's time this young man learned to skinny dip. You told me you used to be an expert at it."

Whatever had darkened David's day washed away as soon as he took the grinning boy from her. Little feet and hands churned the water as squeals of delight rang forth.

As she walked away, David asked, "Where are you going? Put on your bathing suit and join us."

"I'm still mad at you and Nancy for laughing about my cooking. I'll be in the garden pulling weeds."

Nancy had followed her out of the house. She ignored the goad and cast her gaze on the water. "I'll be right there, Mr. David. If I don't take a break, you'll need to put me in a straitjacket."

A loose-fitting shirt, jeans, and work boots comprised CJ's wardrobe change. She made her way to the garden she'd tilled and planted before the trip to Cozumel. Residual frustrations from her day flowed away as she took them out on weeds instead of loved ones. It seemed rewarding to pull up and discard the unwanted invaders that, if left unchecked, would draw the life out of her crops. She wondered if people weren't like garden vegetables and the weeds that infiltrated her carefully spaced rows of composted dirt. The good seeds were beneficial and destined for usefulness in promoting life and joy, while others existed only to harm. The latter seemed useless and better plucked up by their roots, cast off, or burned. She paused and chided herself for uncharitable thoughts about human beings. Still, there was a measure of truth she couldn't deny.

With deep thoughts pushed aside, she busied her hands until the last row of weeds joined a pile and she carried them away in a wheelbarrow. Dirt made black quarter-moons under her fingernails and her back ached from bending over, but it was a good feeling to have accomplished something that needed to be done. After washing off the top layer of dirt from her hands with a garden hose, she allowed them to air dry as she made for the back door. Aromas hit her as soon as she entered. When her stomach growled with hunger, she realized how rushed and meager lunch had been.

Without being asked, David looked up from a skillet and announced, "Hamburger patties, grilled onions, brown gravy, mashed potatoes, and green beans. Sorry, no rolls. You'll have to make do with bread."

She pulled off her boots and left them by the back door before walking to her husband and giving him a good helping of how thankful she was for him keeping them alive with his cooking. The embrace lasted until he untangled her arms. "Let me serve up the gravy before it burns."

Each person, even little Davey, seemed content to eat without conversation. The exercise and change of pace brought the household back into a tentative balance. Still, fatigue and a desire for quiet aloneness was the only dessert anyone seemed to crave. David retreated to his office. Nancy took a yawning child to her bed and lay with him until both fell asleep. CJ washed the supper dishes.

This was her second most favorite time of day. She loved to start her mornings on the back porch swing with her bible and a mug of steaming coffee. After supper, the back-and-forth motion of the swing comforted her in ways she couldn't describe. Sometimes David joined her, but most of the time he found solace in his office. On this night, he joined her.

"Thanks for cleaning up," he said as the swing creaked under his weight.

"It's the least I could do after you cooked such a feast. Did you put a sedative in Nancy and Davey's milk?"

"No need. They could barely keep their eyes open while they ate."

The swing moved at a slow, steady pace. Minutes passed in silence before CJ's curiosity got the better of her. "Why was Captain Crow upset with you today?"

"He's catching heat from up the ladder. The Killeen newspaper published a big story yesterday about the spike of drug and alcohol use by middle school and high school kids. They made a big deal of blaming law enforcement. What prompted the story was an eighth grader who got ahold of moonshine and went joyriding in his parents' pickup. He wrapped it around a telephone pole and is in terrible shape."

She put her hand on David's thigh. "I hadn't heard. When did it happen?"

"Two nights ago. Somehow the reporter learned of the task force. She knows everyone who's been at the meetings."

CJ shook her head. "I haven't received a call. Have you?"

"Not yet, but Captain Crow has." David's hand found hers. "This is another reason I don't want to be a Ranger. Being a lowly sergeant keeps me out of the spotlight."

The swinging continued as Sandy came through the doggy door and settled at their feet with ears up to take in night sounds. "Honey," said CJ. "Is there any way I can skip going to more task force meetings?"

"Why don't you want to be included?"

She leaned into him. As expected, he draped his arm over her shoulder. "It doesn't appear the problem on campus is as bad as we first thought. After talking to the students Lonny made deliveries to, I determined none were into the hard stuff, except maybe one. He's pre-law and surly as the day is long. I wasn't able to get anything out of him, even after threatening to take the video of him to the DA and telling him he'd face disciplinary action from the university. Everyone else fessed up to buying pot or moonshine."

"What are you going to do with the future attorney?"

"Because we didn't recover the drugs, there's not enough to take it to the DA. I turned it over to John. He called Alice and they're having a closed-door session with the young man tomorrow morning. If he doesn't come clean, his days at ACU may soon be over. He'll make it through the semester, but Alice will tell him to find another university."

"You'll be better off without him."

"That's what Alice told John."

Sandy raised her head, yawned, and put it back on her front legs.

"Why not kick him out tomorrow if he doesn't cooperate?" asked David.

CJ stopped the swing. "That has to do with the second reason I don't want to be on the task force. Alice made an off-hand remark this morning about how she needed to avoid any scandals at the university from now till sometime this summer. I think she would appreciate it if I didn't formally associate the university with the task force. Besides, you can keep me informed and I'll pass everything on to John."

The swinging started again. "I can't think of a good reason both of us need to be there."

She patted his leg.

"Do you know why Alice is so worried about a scandal?"

"Beats me, and that doesn't sound like Alice. It was almost like she needs to bide her time." She spoke an afterthought. "Why don't you talk to your dad and find out?"

"It probably has something to do with the regents giving her a hard time. I don't like the idea of asking Dad to snoop."

She believed that might be part of it, but it wasn't the entire story. Or was it? It wouldn't be the first time a group of headstrong regents flexed their muscles. If David didn't want to ask his father, perhaps she'd try to find another way.

David's next question interrupted her thoughts about Alice's motivations. "Anything else exciting happen today?"

She shook her head. "Maria and I made a bunch of students think again about buying pot and moonshine. John took over a lot of my administrative duties so Maria and I can concentrate on keeping dealers away from the campus for the rest of the semester."

David unwrapped his arm, stood, and stretched. He turned around to face her. "What's your gut feeling about how widespread drugs are?"

It took her a few seconds to collect her thoughts. "I said this earlier today, and it's still true. There's a void waiting to be filled. Someone will take Amy and Lonny's place. The big question is, will that person fill it with pot, moonshine, hard drugs, or all three?"

"Do you think there's anyone else in Amy's organization that will step up and take over?"

"I doubt it. They seemed content to pick up a few extra bucks by making simple pot deliveries. What we don't need is someone who's greedy and has no conscience about the dangers of things like crack cocaine, heroin, and especially fentanyl." She rose and duplicated David's stretch. "Did you discover the owner of the car that made the delivery to Lonny yesterday?"

"It took me most of the day, but I finally tracked it down. I'm taking the old farm truck tomorrow and doing surveillance. Hopefully, I'll get photos and video of him making more deliveries. If I do, we'll put a tail on him twenty-four/seven and get a warrant to put a tracker on his car."

She moved in for a hug and goodnight peck that didn't qualify as a kiss. "I'm bushed. Are you coming to bed soon?"

"In a little while."

As she shuffled off to bed, it occurred to her the one thing left unchecked on her list of things to do was talk to Randy. Oh well, that could wait.

CHAPTER FIFTEEN

Sunrise found David backing between white lines of a church parking lot in Harker Heights, a bedroom community near Fort Hood. Many years ago, this sleepy hamlet sat separated from a half-dozen other farm and ranch towns by miles of arid land. That was before the government implemented eminent domain and acquired almost a hundred and sixty thousand acres to the north and turned it into the highest-populated military base in the country. What resulted was the meteoric growth of a patchwork of towns that merged into a quilt-like design of small cities whose boundaries blurred as businesses and housing developments pushed against one another. Harker Heights was one of the irregular-shaped bedroom communities comprising apartment complexes, duplexes, and homes erected with an eye for quantity over quality.

It was the duplex across the street from the church's secondary parking lot and the late model Hyundai Sonata that brought him to this parking spot under the outreaching arms of a live oak tree. He considered the car and thought how well it fit in with the community. Soldiers who inhabited

"

many of the apartments and duplexes wanted something new, but affordable. For many, it was their first new car. What made little sense was the car's inability to transport large quantities of moonshine. Perhaps the delivery to Riverview had been a one-off, a desire of the owner to put his new car through its paces on the interstate.

He raised binoculars and inspected the car. A paper dealer tag explained why he had such trouble tracking the car and its new owner. He wasted hours before he realized the grainy photo of a partial plate was of a new car that hadn't yet posted on the state's database. Armed with the car's description, all it took was a phone call to the dealership in the area and he had what he needed.

He knew it was a long shot to think the owner would be up and out of the duplex this early, but he didn't want to chance missing him. This left him with three sausage biscuits, a thermos of coffee, and a lot of time to think. An hour passed, as did three more. He'd been on enough stake outs to remember to take along a pilot relief bag so he wouldn't have to find a restroom and lose sight of the suspect. At ten o'clock, he was glad he brought it. Five minutes later, a man wearing a skin-tight T-shirt over bulging muscles exited the duplex, climbed into the blue Sonata and squealed tires as he took the corner out of a concrete driveway.

Luckily, the driver kept his driving to something the aging farm truck could keep up with and it wasn't long before he pulled into the parking lot of a gym. David sat in the late morning sun with windows down, hoping for a breath of breeze that didn't come. An hour later, the man exited the gym, threw a bag in the passenger's seat, and drove to a sandwich shop. With each stop, David took photos, but he didn't believe either business was a point of delivery. All the same, he put his phone on record and made a verbal record of the man's activities which included him consuming two sandwiches, a bag of chips, and three refills of something in a tall Styrofoam cup.

At noon the body-builder donned sunglasses and exited the restaurant. He then went back to his duplex, and David backed his truck under the shade of the same tree he'd left earlier. The glamour of working a stake-out diminished as the temperature rose with each passing cloudless hour. He issued a word of thanks to the tree, but scowled at the asphalt from which heat waves made squiggly lines.

Another forty-five minutes and the man walked from the duplex wearing jeans and a loose fitting, short-sleeve cotton shirt with a pink baseball cap atop his close-cropped black hair. The shirt and jeans hid all the tattoos except those from the elbows to the wrists.

The trip through several of the small, interconnected towns brought them to the outskirts of civilization and an industrial park comprised of rows of small, blue-collar businesses. People who repaired things or provided some sort of niche goods or services occupied the nondescript storefronts with mini-warehouses in the back. Intermixed were larger, free-standing buildings, some looking more prosperous than others.

Instead of parking in front, the dealership-new Sonata pulled around back and parked behind a building next to a van with a magnetic advertising sign on the door.

David dared not follow down the gravel and dirt driveway. The business to his right was an auto glass repair shop. He pointed the truck to an open spot between a convertible and a mini-van, facing a chain-link fence. From this vantage point, he could still see the driver as he stepped from his car and disappeared through a back door. He reemerged only seconds later with keys in his hand and unlocked the van parked behind the business. When it became apparent the van was coming his way, David lay flat on the bench seat. He rose in time to crane his neck and get a glimpse of the signage on the van: *Good Times Wholesale Candy Distributors.*

He started the engine. "That explains the lollipops." He backed out of the spot and eased around the building in time to see the van reach blacktop. "It also explains why he drove his new car to Riverview. A van from a candy supplier this far away would draw attention."

The first stop the van made was at a double-wide trailer several miles down a county road. The landscape of junipers, commonly called cedar trees in Central Texas, blocked David from anything but a glimpse of the trailer and made taking photos impossible. He noted the name on the mailbox and the exact location on his cell phone. Whatever was delivered didn't take long.

When the van emerged, it backtracked and headed back in the general direction of Killeen. Six more stops followed, the first on the side of a dollar store. Unlike the last delivery, he could see the cardboard boxes being transferred from the candy van to the trunk of an older Cadillac. He noted the transfer occurred after Muscle Man received a brown envelope. Five boxes went into the cavernous trunk, four of which strained the skinny arms of the woman taking delivery. The last box seemed light in comparison.

The next stop was in Copperas Cove, not far off Highway190. The transaction took place in back of a convenience store, tucked down a secondary street, close to the high school. Photos were out of the question because of the small parking lot, but David knew a transaction had occurred when the van rounded the corner of the store and an aging Dodge emerged from the other direction coughing a trail of blue smoke from its tailpipe.

One more stop and delivery took place behind a dry cleaner on the west side of Killeen.

The van then worked its way onto Highway 190. It traveled east until the sign for the main entrance to Fort Hood came into view. The van's blinker flashed. "He wouldn't dare," whispered David. The delivery driver soon proved him wrong. David pulled off the road before he reached a point of no return and watched. The van pulled to the front gate and stopped. It took only seconds before the soldier guarding the post motioned the vendor to pass. David considered following, but then thought better of it. By the time he answered the guard's questions, the van would disappear in the vast network of roads. Instead, he pulled a U-turn, went back to 190, found a place where he could see eastbound traffic and waited.

An hour melted into two and so did David under the relentless sun. It occurred to him Fort Hood had multiple security gates for Muscle Man to choose from. It was more likely the van wouldn't come this way.

His day was through except for two more things to check before he traveled back to Riverview. The hot wind whipped his shirt sleeve and did a better-than-nothing job of cooling him as he returned to the candy company. He drove slowly past the back side of the building where Muscle Man's van was. What David hadn't counted on were two more vans parked beside it. The candy company could be legit, with a side business of drugs that was the real money maker.

His next stop was a Whataburger restaurant where he loaded up on a very late lunch of a double-meat cheeseburger with jalapenos, fries, and multiple glasses of sweet iced tea. The day hadn't been perfect, but productive all the same. It would be a late night of filling out reports, sending e-mails, and making phone calls. The ball was rolling, and his thoughts turned to home. Another dip in the pool sounded better than anything he could think of.

———

WHEN CJ PULLED AWAY from the university to go home, she found herself following David. A wave of nostalgia swept over her at the sight of him driving the Ford F-150 she brought into their marriage. It had been her father's truck, and she'd treated it with tender loving care throughout high school, college, and ten years into her career in law enforcement. She could still see the look of pride on her father's face when he finally bought his first, and last, new truck. She was in middle school when a drunk driver crossed the double yellow line and ended the life of the deputy sheriff, the man she called Daddy.

She parked under the carport while David allowed the farm truck to sleep where it normally did, on the side of the barn. She waited to go in until he caught up with her.

"Where's Nancy?" he asked with no other preliminary greeting.

"Staying late at the library. Bea picked up Davey from the early childhood development center this afternoon. I told her about you swimming with him last night and her eyes lit up. She said the three of them would have a skinny-dipping party this evening."

David's eyebrows rose. "I don't know about you, but I could use a long swim."

She placed her hand on his back to direct him inside, but drew it away. "Your shirt is sopping wet."

"Everything on that old truck works except the air conditioner."

"It's not supposed to. It's a farm truck." She thought about his offer to cool off in the pool. "Are you really going swimming?"

"Yep. Where's my bathing suit?"

"In the third drawer of your dresser, where it always lives."

"Are you going to join me?" He stopped and pulled her to

him. "Since we're all alone, we could have our own pool party."

CJ grinned. "That sounds good, but I'm bushed. Give me a rain check on that offer."

"Alright, but you'll miss a good time."

"Now, tell me about your day."

David could be concise, yet thorough, and usually was. He began his tale when he arrived in the church parking lot and ended when he drove back by the duplex and found the muscled-up alcohol and drug dealer's car back at the condo.

CJ trailed David back through the house. She considered the progress he'd made and opened with a question. "Three vans? Do you think each one delivers moonshine and drugs?"

"That's my theory. The guy I followed worked the west part of the county and part of Fort Hood."

"You don't think he worked it all?"

"There are a lot of businesses on base. I think he made some legitimate candy deliveries, and some that weren't. The three vans all look the same, and Fort Hood is huge, with over fifty thousand troops stationed there. Vendors come and go all the time. It's like another city unto itself."

After doing some quick math in her head, CJ turned to David. "Three vans making multiple deliveries every day add up to a lot of drugs and moonshine."

Once outside, David sat on one of the pool's concrete steps and splashed with his feet. "It's possible they use the other two vans just for legitimate deliveries. It's also possible that other businesses are doing something similar but answer to the same key guy. There's a ton of work for people to follow up on."

"Including you?"

"I hope not. I spoke with Captain Crow on the way home. He seemed more inclined to have me make a presentation to the task force and let the cities and county take over the tedious work of surveillance and building the case."

She hoped they had both done their part in gathering evidence, but doubted that would be the end of their involvement. Another question crossed her mind. "How high in the organization is the guy you trailed today?"

"Mid-level at most. Looks to have more muscles than brains. He should have spotted me on at least two occasions. The people he delivered to are most likely street-level dealers. I watched him work all day. He's useful as an intimidating collector, but he's too careless to be very high up."

He ducked under the water and came out slicking back his hair. "How was your day? Productive?"

"Not very productive. John's graduate assistant went to the hospital with some sort of staph infection. That puts things back the way they were with John teaching and keeping office hours half time and me with no one to take over my regular duties. Maria and I are trying to work our sources. She stayed at it all day and said everything is quiet. No mention of fentanyl or lollipops."

"That's good news. Lonny's quick arrest may have made the guys in Killeen think twice before expanding this far south."

She turned her head. "Do you really think so?"

"No, but you might have bought some time."

CHAPTER SIXTEEN

Peter Starks and Maria arrived in CJ's office as she pushed a solvent-soaked cleaning patch through the barrel of her pistol. Maria covered a smile as he slowed his pace and stared at the weapon.

CJ waved him to the seat in front of her desk as if cleaning a pistol was the most natural thing for anyone to do. "Come on in, Peter. Don't mind the pistol. I had to play range master at the annual pistol competition this morning. I couldn't help but put some holes in paper myself." Pushing the firearm and cleaning kit to the side, she folded her hands and waited for him to speak.

"Detective Vasquez said you wanted to see me?"

CJ nodded and took measure of the young man wearing canvas boat shoes, cranberry-colored pleated shorts, and a checked monogrammed shirt with the shirttail out. He had a thick head of hair, and up close it became even more apparent how much effort he put into grooming. Waves of milk-chocolate brown swept in multiple directions, including a patch that fell across his left eyebrow. It reminded her of film clips she'd seen of former President Kennedy. He pushed it up with a practiced movement and smiled with teeth that seemed a half-size too large and two shades too white. "How can I help you?"

"That's refreshing," said CJ after delivering a smile of her own. She had to admit, Peter was both charming and disarming with how comfortable he looked in what should have been a stressful situation. "Most of the students I talk to aren't so accommodating, or at ease, when they come to my office."

His smile broadened. "I'm training myself to be at ease in any situation. This is perfect. I never expected to be looking at a 9mm Glock when I walked in." He leaned forward. "Tell me, how did I react?"

"It's a .40 cal, not a 9mm. As for your reaction, you did much better than most people your age. I'll give you a score of ninety on maintaining your pace and an eighty on controlling your eyes. I could see a full ring of white around both brown pupils, but you made a fast recovery."

He slapped his leg. "Darn. I'll need to work on that."

Her smile stayed in place until she said, "I want to talk to you about Amy Sneller."

It's unnatural to smile and swallow at the same time. Peter did a better job at trying to do it than most, but his Adam's apple bobbed.

"That name doesn't ring a bell." He paused. "Wait. Didn't I hear or read something about a female student being murdered? Was that her?"

"Amy was a graduate student. They found her body below the dam of a lake about an hour north of Riverview. The reason I'm asking is that I saw you talking to her at the Campus Grind before spring break. We're asking anyone who knew her to help Bell County investigators with their investigation."

A thatch of hair fell to his eyebrow as he shook his head.

This time he let it stay where it was. "Sorry, but I won't be any help to them. To tell the truth, I talk to a lot of students at the Grind. It's another part of my training. I'm a business major and I want to get into sales after I graduate. It's about getting to know people and providing them with something that fills a want or a need in their lives. Talking to so many people is helping me develop a spreadsheet of potential customers for when I graduate. As for this Amy person, I didn't know her name until you told me."

"Are you sure? It looked to me like Amy didn't want to talk to you. In fact, she became quite animated."

His nod carried an air of self-assurance. "Exactly. Part of approaching people and trying to get to know them is knowing some will reject me. That's the part of sales that most people can't cope with. I'm using my time in college to overcome my fear of rejection by placing myself in situations where I'm guaranteed to get rejected." He reached for his back pocket and drew out a wallet. "To make sure, I had these two cards printed up."

CJ examined the business cards. One described him as a recruiter for an organization that advocated government seizure of all firearms. The second called for open carry with no restrictions.

"I'm pretty good at reading people," said Peter with a note of pride. "I find people who strike me as having extreme views on the gun debate or some other hot-button topic, then I try to convince them to support something I know is opposite of what they believe. It hones my sales skills and ensures they'll reject me."

CJ couldn't deny the logic of what he was saying, but didn't want to fall for his smooth rhetoric. "Do you even remember meeting Amy?"

"I remember having a conversation with a girl who dressed like she'd made a haul from Goodwill and had ink all down her arm. She never gave me the time of day, let alone her name."

The dead end couldn't have been more obvious if he'd held up a street sign. She'd run out of questions concerning Amy, but there was one more thing to explore. She locked her gaze on Maria, a pre-arranged signal that she was to take over.

"I guess that explains why you were talking with Randy McNutt yesterday at the Grind."

Peter's gaze cast to the ceiling. "McNutt? Was that his last name? I only know him as Randy. I wrote him off as a potential future customer."

"Why did you do that?"

He shifted his gaze between Maria and CJ. "I don't eliminate many people, but someone like Randy will never amount to much. I'm not sure what I'm going to sell, but I'm targeting those with the potential to be mid-six figure and higher earners. If you want to get rich, which I do, you need to surround yourself with people who either have the money to get you there, or will have it. That leaves Randy out."

CJ wanted to stick up for Randy, but not make it too obvious. "What makes you think Randy won't be successful?"

Peter leaned back. "He's dropping out and not coming back. Said he'd rather work as a mechanic somewhere in town."

It was CJ's turn to have wide eyes and swallow. She sat in silence as she wondered if David's decision to kick him out and Bob dismissing him led Randy to make a rash decision.

"Is that all?" asked Peter.

The question brought her back to the here and now. "One more question," said CJ. "Because you talk to so many students, are you hearing anything about moonshine?"

He didn't seem fazed in the least. "I saw a lot of that stuff on South Padre during spring break, but it's a non-issue to me. I never drink alcohol of any kind."

CJ nodded and rose to her feet with right hand extended and he gave it a confident shake. She issued a parting invitation. "Thanks for coming in. You're in a unique position to hear things that might interest us. Call me or Detective Vasquez any time if you come across something a couple of cops might be interested in."

His smile and charm could melt frozen butter. "Only if you allow me to put your name on my spreadsheet."

"Go ahead, but whatever you end up selling better have something to do with farming or ranching."

He issued a soft laugh as he turned to leave. "I haven't considered that, but it's possible. They're not making any more land and people will always need to eat. Like I said, find the want or need and meet it."

They waited until his footsteps faded. Maria stuck her head in the hall to make sure he'd left before she came back in and shut the door.

"Well?" asked CJ.

"You know me. I don't trust anyone."

A grin crept across CJ's face. "Would you buy a used car from him?"

"No. But I'd consider going on a test drive in a new one just to look at his hair." Maria paused. "Was he telling the truth about Amy?"

CJ waited a couple of seconds before responding. "I think he was telling the truth ninety-nine percent of the time. It's the other one percent that concerns me. The best liars are those who tell the truth as often as they can."

"What was he lying about?"

Shoulders rose and fell. "Maybe nothing, but I'm going to find out today if Randy is dropping out."

"Do you want me to do a background check on Peter?"

"Don't make it a priority." She cast a squinting gaze at

Maria. "Are you looking for an excuse to look at his picture every day?"

Maria rose. "It would never work out between us."

"Why not? I saw the way he looked at you."

Her raven hair glistened as she shook her head. "My bank balance doesn't meet his standards, and it's unlikely it ever will. Did you notice he didn't ask to add me to his spreadsheet of future clients?"

Maria was out the door before CJ could think of a snappy comeback. Then it occurred to her that Peter might have known about her and David's financial situation, which put them well within Peter's parameters. She dismissed the thought and wondered where she might find Randy. The growl her stomach made put Randy on the back burner. She'd stop by his trailer on the way home.

THE THREE CALLS she made to Randy's cell phone went directly to voice mail, the first after five rings and the next two after only one ring. That meant he received the calls and chose not to answer. As she drove down the gravel road, his trailer appeared in the distance with his rebuilt Dodge Charger resting near the front porch.

She'd never been to the trailer sitting on a five-acre mini-ranch. Randy may have been a wiz in repairing cars, but she could only describe his home as a dump. Not that surprising, considering Randy's father was a confirmed alcoholic who spent as much time behind bars as on the free side of them. Still, she expected better of Randy based on Bob telling her how fastidious he was about keeping his work area clean and his tools in their proper place.

The trailer, however, was a different story. Skirting on the two-toned silver and beige single wide looked like a crack addict's teeth. The panels that hung on were stained brown with mud that splashed from a yard dotted with unambitious clumps of grass. The front porch groaned under her steps, and any railing that might have once been there was nowhere in sight. A box fan sat in the living room window, drawing warm air into the shoe-box shaped dwelling.

A wave of guilt swept over her. She and David could have been more forgiving. The feeling didn't last long when she reconsidered. David and Bob were right. Randy's poor decisions earned consequences. He'd violated their home, and if given the chance, would have violated Nancy, perhaps against her will. Was this the justice they'd sought when Randy began a chain of events that caused her to lose her daughter?

She squared her shoulders and gave the metal door three firm raps. He must have seen her coming because the door opened as soon as the echo of the third knock ended.

Randy looked as he always did, except he'd discarded his tennis shoes beside a couch covered with a dingy sheet. His dark hair was matted on the sides, which told her he'd had on a cap until recently. Not surprising. He almost always wore a baseball cap of some sort. The only question was, would he wear it with the bill facing the front or the back?

He backed away from the door and allowed her to pass, saying nothing. The awkwardness of the moment made the air thick, which wasn't helped by the fan pushing around late afternoon heat. She couldn't imagine how oppressive the heat would be in mid-summer.

Instead of beating around the bush, she got right to the point. "I heard today that you're dropping your classes. Is that right?"

"You heard right." He pointed to a chair. "Want to sit down?"

She took the offer and settled into one of the mismatched kitchen chairs that had found its way into the living room.

From the condition of the other furniture, it looked like the safest option. "Want to tell me why?"

He plopped down on a massive bean-bag patched with duct tape before he answered. "I finally quit kidding myself and wasting my time. I can make ten times as much working as a mechanic or restoring old cars than as a night janitor at ACU. I proved that working with Mr. Bob."

"Did you know he's building a garage and then a house on the land at our place?"

"Yeah, he told me."

"He might have some work for you after it's finished."

He shook his head in such a way that said he'd settled the issue in his mind.

"Look, Randy. I know we had an awful night, but—"

He cut her off with a wave of the hand. "You've got it all wrong. I have nothing against any of you. It was my fault and I take responsibility for everything that happened. Mr. David was right in tossing me out. I'll never forget the kindness you showed me by paying the hospital bill, buying me clothes, and giving me a place to live when I needed it. You treated me right, and I blew it."

CJ pulled her hair back. "Then why did you say you'll not work with Mr. Bob?"

"It's the same reason I quit college. I don't belong."

She opened her mouth to serve up a platitude, but he cut her off again. "It's true. I'm not failing any of my classes, so I know I could make it through college if I wanted to. That's the problem. I don't want to. For me, it would be silly to get so far in debt that I'd spend the next twenty years paying off student loans doing some office job I hated. I work with my hands. It's what I like and what I'm good at."

It was clear she could keep chopping, but no wood chips were flying. She nodded and stood to leave. "I wanted to stop by and make sure you weren't making a mistake by not finishing the semester. Do you have a job lined up yet?"

"No worries on that front. Good mechanics are hard to find."

She couldn't argue with that, so she waited for him to continue.

"Until then, I have a list of people wanting me to work on their cars and trucks. I can do that here in the barn. That will help me decide if I want to work for someone else or strike out on my own."

"Do you have enough tools and equipment to do that?"

"I have plenty to get started." He stood and moved toward the door.

CJ started to bid him goodbye but got choked on her inhale. All manner of unladylike sounds came forth while trying to get her breath, and voice, back.

"You must have swallowed a gnat," said Randy. Meanwhile, he had water running in the kitchen sink and brought her a glass. She washed her mouth out with the first swig. The next three swallows went down. After examining the clarity of the water, she said, "This is wonderful. You must have a deep well."

"It's the only thing my dad didn't skimp on. He made sure they drilled all the way down into the aquifer."

"We tied into a rural water system. Big mistake in not drilling a well. Our water's not near as good as this."

She bid him goodbye again and headed home. Randy might not be the most trustworthy young man she'd ever met, and he was prone to making impulsive decisions, but he was a hard worker and shrewd in his own way. She needn't worry about him making a living.

As she turned off the blacktop to their farm, she remembered she hadn't asked Randy about his meeting with Peter Starks. It didn't matter. Peter had written Randy off, and

Randy was traveling down a completely different road. They'd probably never see each other again.

The faces of Holly Grimes and Amy Sneller came to her with a clarity that startled her. Two young women had met early and needless deaths, and she had done nothing today to push the investigations forward. It was to be expected, but she never liked it when an investigation stalled.

Her mood changed when she crossed over the cattle guard to their property. Things always looked better on this side of the fence.

CHAPTER SEVENTEEN

As CJ came from their bedroom, her phone vibrated in the back pocket of her jeans. "Hello, handsome. Are you headed home yet?"

"On my way. How does Mexican food sound tonight?"

She didn't have to think before answering. "A lot better than a cold sandwich."

"I'm thirty minutes out. Meet me at La Hacienda."

Her mouth watered at the mere thought of their favorite Tex-Mex food.

As usual, the close-in parking lot couldn't accommodate her. She drove to a massive back lot and wheeled her SUV into an open space. Aromas of seasoned, grilled flank steak, and cooked onions with bell peppers hit her and intensified as she closed the distance on the restaurant. The salad she ate at the Grind was nothing but a faded memory.

Once inside, she waited with David for ten minutes until a dark-eyed hostess called out, "Harper. Your table is ready." They followed the maiden to a table for four. Their server soon arrived with a basket of chips and two kinds of salsa.

"You made good time getting here," said CJ.

"No wrecks on the interstate for a change."

Drinks arrived and the server informed them of the daily special.

"I know what I want," said David. He looked at CJ and waited for a response.

"Fajitas for me, too."

David tucked his thumb into his palm and held up his hand. "We'll have the fajitas for four." The server nodded and went to place the order. "That way we'll have left-overs for Nancy."

It occurred to her that during their year of marriage, she and David had reached the point they didn't need as many words to communicate as they once did. Over eight years of working together as highway patrol officers aided the telepathy.

With the order placed, she continued with their normal, abbreviated way of starting an evening's conversation on a day when they'd gone their separate ways. "Whose turn is it?"

"You go first."

She nodded. "Pistol competition this morning. Maria came in second, behind Lieutenant Grimes. This afternoon I interviewed a student named Peter Starks. I noticed him trying to talk to Amy Sneller before spring break. She gave him the brush off."

David scooped red salsa on a wedge of tortilla chip but waited to send it into his mouth. "Anything to it?"

"He's a slick operator, but I don't think so. Gave me a story of how he wants to go into sales after he graduates. For now, he picks out people he knows will shut him down, just so he can overcome fear of rejection."

"That's a new one," said David. "Someone willing to get rejected on purpose could probably sell sand to Dubai." He cocked his head. "Tell me he didn't sell you something."

"Not yet, but he wanted to add my name to his spread sheet of potential future customers."

David shoved in another chip, this time loaded down with *salsa verdé*. He waited until he downed it before going on, which gave her a chance to grab a chip and dip it in red sauce.

"Why doesn't Peter sell something now?"

She shrugged. "Maybe he does. Either that or he's a trust fund baby."

"Why do you say that?"

"His clothes are all designer brands, and the Rolex on his wrist looked real."

"Red flags didn't go up for you?"

"Only one little-bitty one and Maria was no help. She's still at the point of assuming everyone is guilty until proven innocent. I think Peter is a rich kid who wants to get even richer."

The server came, topped off their water, and told them their order would be out soon.

The break gave CJ time to think about how David might react to her going to see Randy. She relayed the story and waited.

"It sounds to me like he made a poor short-term decision and a good long-term one. He already had the semester paid for and you said he's passing. Why throw away all that money when he could have stuck it out and had something to show for it?"

"I guess he wants to earn money now."

David shook his head in a way that said he thought the decision was irresponsible. "And you say he doesn't want to work with Dad?"

"That's what he told me. He's trying to decide if he wants to start his own business or work for someone in town."

David's eyebrows pinched together. "Were you so

concerned about him you had to go by and try to talk him into staying in college?"

"That's only part of it. I saw him and Peter Starks talking in the Campus Grind yesterday. It made little sense until Peter told me he tries to talk to all kinds of people. He didn't use these words, but he wrote Randy off as a loser that didn't make the cut for his prospect list."

David opened his mouth to speak. She raised her eyebrows, a clue he didn't need to say anything deprecating about Randy. She'd learned the expression from her mother.

"What? I was going to say we need to stop by Dad's and see if he knows Randy won't be coming back to work for him when his barn is complete."

"Uh-huh. Sure you were." She picked up another chip. "Your turn. What did you do today?"

The words came in a torrent. "Captain Crow arranged a meeting of the task force this morning. I gave him a report of what I discovered yesterday and showed him the photos and video I took. We broke for lunch. After that, we came back to the office and worked out a plan for surveillance that included all local departments and Fort Hood."

CJ held up a hand. "Slow down. You changed pronouns on me. First you said him, then we. Was someone else in on the meeting with Captain Crow?"

"Blake was there. After the meeting, I drove home. Where's our food?"

"That's it? No details?"

"One more thing. Do you remember Holly Grimes' uncle, Pancho?"

She had to think for a minute. "Oh yeah. He was the guy with the big scar on his head that was talking with Billy Paul. Didn't he get wounded in Afghanistan?"

"That's him. Captain Crow says he calls almost every day,

wanting to know if we've found the people responsible for Holly's death. Has he been calling you?"

"No."

A cloud of smoke followed the server as she arrived with a sizzling, black cast iron platter on a wooden tray. The fajitas and vegetables continued to cook as husband and wife pushed the chips and salsas out of the center of the table. A second server arrived with plates of refried beans, Spanish rice, shredded lettuce, diced tomatoes, sour cream, and a stack of flour tortillas in a container to keep them piping hot. All talk of work ceased.

CHANGES HAD TAKEN place in Bob's house since CJ last visited, which included the addition of a second desk to his office. She only saw it from a distance, but thought it odd that her father-in-law had added a second desk to go along with the existing one and his drafting table. Another change was that Alice opened the door and greeted them wearing house shoes.

Bob emerged from the kitchen and met them with arms spread open.

"This is an unexpected pleasure," said Alice. "Please tell me you're not the bearer of bad news."

"Nothing like that," said CJ. "La Hacienda sounded better than sandwiches."

Alice's eyes sparked even more than usual. "I could eat there every night." She led the way into the living room.

"Aah," David sat in a wing-back chair with legs extended, right boot over the left. "Feels good to relax."

Their hostess had no more sat down before she stood again. "Where are my manners? You'll want coffee and a little something sweet to top off your meal. We have sherbet and some delicious French macaroons." She raised her hands as CJ leaned forward to stand. "I'll get it. Won't take but a minute."

It seemed strange to be waited on by her boss's boss. It also struck her as odd that Alice seemed so at home in Bob's house.

Bob waited until Alice left before he turned to David. "Now that she's gone, you two can tell me why you really stopped by."

David feigned offense, but did a lousy job of selling it. "Can't a son come see his father and not have some other motive?"

"It's a remote possibility, but I doubt it. You both work way too many hours, have two homicides to solve, and you're trying to keep the lid on moonshine and deadly drugs. Your bellies are full of Mexican food and if I was you, I'd be home with my feet up and watch television for six minutes before I fell sound sleep."

"We're busted," said CJ. "We came to give you a report on Randy. He's dropping out of school and said he doesn't plan to work with you after you get your barn built."

Bob leaned back and tapped his lips with an index finger. After he'd digested the news, he asked, "Did he give a reason for these sudden changes?"

"He said he didn't belong in college and that he might start his own business or work in town."

"Good."

The response came without a hint of malice, but the suddenness of it took her by surprise all the same. "Why do you say that?"

"Randy has a healthy measure of ambition, but he's prone to make rash decisions and bite off more than he can chew. He pressured me to buy several old muscle cars and work a lot more than I wanted to. I'm looking at my car restoration business as a hobby, something I can work on when I want, not living up to his expectations and being worried about him overspending money that isn't his."

David spoke up. "You sound like you don't trust him."

Bob shrugged. "He's honest enough, I guess."

"You don't sound so sure."

"For sixteen years I lived alongside men that had grand ideas about how they were going to get rich. Listening to them made me a confirmed skeptic about people who want too much, too fast. He's young and impulsive. I've decided if I do have people working with me, it will be those who've been around a while and don't pressure me."

CJ rose from the couch. "I'm going to see if I can give Alice a hand."

The coffee pot sputtered out the last drops when she walked into the kitchen. Alice had already plated a dozen multicolored French macaroons and had small glass bowls set out for sherbet. She spoke as she opened the freezer door on the side-by-side. "You'll find the mugs one cabinet to the left of the sink."

When CJ sat the mugs on the granite counter, she noticed a delicate porcelain bowl sitting next to the sink. In the bowl sat two gold rings, a man's and a woman's. She did a double take. When she cast her gaze toward the freezer door, Alice was staring at her with a definite deer-in-the-headlights look.

Not knowing what else to say, CJ asked, "Is there something David and I don't know about?"

Alice put the sherbet back in the freezer. "We'd better join the men before we have our desert." She moved to the living room and stood to Bob's side, leaned down and said, "She saw the rings."

He nodded and smiled like he'd won the lottery. "Good. All this secrecy isn't any way to live."

David cast an inquiring gaze to his father. "Something

tells me I'll be glad I'm already seated. Did I hear Alice say 'rings'?"

Bob nodded.

"As in wedding rings?"

Alice nodded and smiled.

CJ squealed and moved to enfold Alice in a hug. "That's wonderful. When's the wedding?" Her mind moved into a gear she didn't know existed. She pictured herself helping Alice pick out a dress, enlist Aunt Bea to help decorate the chapel at the university, and plan the reception. She'd gone so deep into her thoughts she almost missed Bob's delayed answer to CJ's question about the timing of the wedding.

"We eloped when you were in Cozumel."

David shot to his feet, dragged his father from his chair, and gave him a bear hug that included back slaps.

CJ stood with mouth hinged open. The only thing that squeaked out was, "No big wedding?"

Alice took her by the hands. "Only Bea and Billy Paul know. They were our two witnesses."

Bob joined Alice and drew her close. "Randy isn't the only impulsive guy around."

David howled. CJ tried to recover by giving both a hug and fought not to be offended.

Bob gave her and David a hard look. "It's important that no one finds out about this until after the semester ends."

"Why not?" asked David.

Alice answered for him. "As you're aware, there's a contingent of regents that believes the university needs new leadership as soon as possible. They may be right, but I want to stay until at least the end of the semester and preferably through the summer. Some very influential people have approached me to run for state representative. Our current representative has health issues and plans on leaving before his term has expired. The governor wants me to fill the unexpired term if our representative can't fulfill his term. After that, I'll see if it suits me. If so, I'll try to stay at it. If not, I'll ease into retirement and see where that leads. There is one catch. There can't be any hint of a scandal. Bob will go with me to the June regents meeting, where we'll tell them about our marriage. They should stop sharpening their knives if the university is relatively drug and alcohol free and I'm still morally acceptable."

"This is cause for a celebration," said David.

Alice took the hint. "Coffee, sherbet, and macaroons await us in the kitchen."

With her emotions having gone through the spin cycle, CJ tried to regain her balance as she trailed Alice to the kitchen.

Alice slowed, slipped her hand in CJ's arm, and said, "Please forgive me. We didn't mean to hurt you two, or anyone else."

A practical question came to her mind. "How are you and Bob keeping the marriage hidden?"

"He's busy building the barn and drafting the plans for our home. Lord knows I'm booked every day, and I never spend the night here."

It didn't take long before CJ's emotions did a U-turn and a sense of joy and celebration came over her. She smiled. "I'm happy for you, really I am, but I can't imagine the university without you."

"I'll miss it, if I have to leave. It's strange how liberated and alive I feel. I don't know if it's because I have someone to share my life or I realize there are more choices available to me."

CJ considered how quickly her world was changing. In a few months, the university would know if they were getting a new president. How much could happen in that amount of time?

CHAPTER EIGHTEEN

Lifting his gaze from the mounds of printouts accumulated on the desk in his home office, David rubbed his eyes.

"Did you stay up all night?" asked CJ.

"I came to bed about one-thirty and got up early. Slow progress, and Captain Crow isn't smiling."

He enjoyed the feel of the pre-dawn hug she gave him as she leaned down and whisper-tickled his ear.

"I rarely associate happy with Captain Crow." She reached and picked up a file. "I see you finally got the full forensics report from Amy's murder. What did it take? Three weeks?"

"Yeah. They don't process DNA at the speed they show on television. The lab's backed up, and I had to stand on some desks to get it this quick."

She flipped pages, scanned them, and then closed the file. "It's too early to read this. Bring me up to speed."

"Cops in various towns have kept Mr. Muscles and a couple of other drivers for the candy company under constant surveillance. Scrapings from under Amy's fingernails show DNA from someone other than the guy I followed. There isn't a match in the database. That means her killer, or someone associated with killing her, is one of those pesky unknown persons." He motioned with his fingers to put air quotes around the words *unknown persons*. "The good news is, we can rule out a lot of groups, including military and law enforcement, and many criminals. They are all in the database."

"Are you sure the DNA didn't belong to Mr. Muscles?"

"I checked. He received a dishonorable discharge from Fort Hood. That eliminates him."

CJ placed her hand over her mouth to stifle an early morning yawn. She picked up the photo of the car David had followed to the candy business. "Looks brand new."

"He bought it two days before I followed him. Paid half down in cash."

"Sounds like he earned a big bonus."

David didn't respond, but a puzzle piece appeared in his mind that looked like it might fit into a couple of others. He rose and gave his wife a full kiss on the lips. "You're amazing."

She took a step back. "You have that funny look in your eye again. The one where you discover how to untangle a hard problem."

"I'll cook while you listen." With the truncated invitation to breakfast issued, he made for the kitchen. Upon arrival he retrieved pancake mix, eggs, milk, and a pound of sausage.

As CJ perched on a bar stool on the other side of the counter, he talked as he worked. "We know Amy went to the hotel in Killeen, but didn't check in. The parking lot is where we found her car. Most likely, someone picked her up or abducted her there. Right?"

She nodded.

"We also know Mr. Muscles paid half in cash for a new car days after someone killed her."

CJ nodded and added, "It wasn't his DNA under Amy's fingernail."

"True, but what if he was the driver? What if her killer was in the car, too?"

CJ didn't look convinced.

He continued slicing a tube of sausage into patties. "I know it's a long shot, but no one thought to trace the vehicle Muscles traded in. If I can find it, there might be some trace of DNA that matches what we already have."

CJ rose and poured herself a cup of coffee. "I'd say your chances are about a hundred to one, but that's better than what you have now."

He looked at the clock on the microwave. "I want to be at the dealership as soon as they open."

DAVID'S WORDS to the salesman were brief. "I need to see the owner."

The man wore a shirt identical to three others waiting for the first customers to appear at the dealership. "He won't be in for another hour. The sales manager is here." He pointed to the only office next to the sales floor that had a door.

David nodded, walked past a covey of gleaming cars, and took a step inside the open door. The silver badge on his shirt and pistol on his hip was enough to get the woman's attention. She had short, curly black hair sprinkled with gray, mocha skin and a clean desk. Photos of family and one of her in an officer's dress uniform adorned a shelf behind her.

Following introductions, the former captain gave him a sideways look. "Harper? Were you ever in the Middle East?"

He nodded. "Scout sniper."

"You had quite a reputation, Sgt. Harper. I was in personnel and remember your file. It was thicker than most, and not because of disciplinary infractions." She showed a smile and asked, "What can I do for you?"

"Two weeks ago, on a Saturday, a customer bought a new Sonata here. I need to know if you took a vehicle in trade, and if so, do you still have it?"

"Give me his name, and I'll look it up." She brought her computer to life and typed with practiced speed.

When he gave the name, her countenance changed. "I remember him. Big guy. Bought a blue Sonata and put a lot of cash down. He didn't haggle about the price. It doesn't surprise me someone working with the Rangers is interested in him."

"Dishonorable discharge from Hood a few years back," confided David.

"No surprise there, either." She continued typing. "There it is. He traded in a Crown Vic." She continued to tap on her keyboard. "He bought it at a police auction. I remember it now. It still had the searchlight mounted on the driver's side. It looked like a cop car, black and white paint scheme and everything but the lights on top."

"Is it still here?"

Her head shook. "Way too many miles and not enough meat left on the bones. It went straight to auction." She continued typing. "I'll write the address and phone number for you. It's the auto auction between Temple and Waco. I can't tell you if they still have it. Probably not. They have sales every Wednesday, so I doubt it."

After a few more exchanges of pleasantries, he was on his way to Temple and a multi-acre slab of asphalt with cars and trucks that ran the range from good bargains to relics destined for salvage yards.

The manager of the auto auction had a belly that hid his belt buckle. He chewed the soggy end of a cigar and walked slough-footed. His face was both florid and lined with tiny broken blood vessels. David hoped he could extract information before the man dropped over from a coronary or stroke.

"I'd be happy to help ya'," said the man. "But Sue Ann keeps track of all the title transfers and she had to run to the bank. She'll be back before long if she doesn't get to talking. She's got a mind of her own, but she knows titles like nobody I've ever seen."

David could usually be patient, but not when he was hot on a trail. "Do you sell every car that comes here? Even those that don't run?"

The manager took the cigar out of his mouth for the third time. "All depends if the seller has a reserve on it or not. A car like you're talking about is almost sure to sell, especially if it made it to the auction line under its own power."

"I understand you don't clean the cars before you sell them. Is that right?"

"That's the seller's responsibility. Some come in looking showroom new and others aren't worth the water, soap and time it would take to give them a bath."

"Do you mind if I drive through the lot to see if I can spot it?"

"Help yourself. Should be easy enough to spot." The cigar went back in the manager's mouth.

With the auction only a day away, the rows of vehicles looked like the parking lot of a mall at Christmas. Cars and trucks of every shape, size and description lined up awaiting buyers to determine if they could make a profit on them or not. It took ten minutes of slow driving before a scan of the last row proved to be a fruitless search.

Returning to the office, David had better luck as the cigar chewer introduced him to Sue Ann, a thin woman with blue hair and keen eyes magnified by lenses of plastic-framed glasses. Both her attire and desk were neat. Despite her age, which he judged to be pushing eighty, Sue Ann moved with speed and no wasted motion. There was no doubt who really ran the business.

After receiving the new car dealership's name and date the car arrived at the auction, she stepped to a file cabinet and withdrew a thick file folder. She opened it, licked her finger and flipped pages. Without fanfare, she announced, "Sold to AA Used Cars in Temple. Is there any other information you require?"

"You've been a great help. Thank you."

Once back in his SUV, he located the used car lot, placed a call, and received the information he hoped for. "Yes, sir. She's still here and ready for a test drive. Still got a lot of good miles on her and great tires."

"I'm on my way."

What David didn't tell the man was he was inviting Bell County homicide detectives and a tow truck to join him. The Crown Vic would leave the used car lot today, but not the way the man he talked to was hoping.

The two detectives were waiting for him when he arrived. The senior of the two in age extended a hand. "Glad you called, Sgt. Harper. We were getting nowhere fast in our investigation."

"This is a long shot, but if it pans out, it should put you back on the trail."

The trio walked to a portable building sitting on a gravel parking lot dotted with about thirty vehicles, each looking the worse for wear. Placards under the windshield wipers boasted sales pitches offering special financing, reliability, and the lowest prices in town. The black and white Ford Crown Victoria sat on the second row, its chrome search light shining in the sun. Water spots on the side windows told David the car had been washed, but not dried with care.

"Howdy! Did one of you call about the Crown Vic?"

The man's countenance changed from a toothy smile to a

scowl when all three spun and he beheld three badges and the same number of pistols.

"We'll need the keys," said the senior detective.

The man nodded. "Brought 'em with me."

David withdrew latex gloves from the pocket of his western-cut slacks, put them on and took the keys. "I see you washed it. Did you clean the interior?"

"Didn't need it when I bought it. All I did was spray her with an air freshener that has a new-car smell."

"What about the trunk?"

"It's as is, except I took out the spare. I sell those as an add-on after I get the customer to commit to buying."

David walked around to the back of the car, fit the key in the lock and twisted. The trunk sprung open and all three lawmen looked inside, but didn't touch. The younger detective put his hands on his knees and bent over to get a better look. "That stain could be blood."

The senior detective turned to the owner. "A car hauler is on the way. We'll be impounding this vehicle and I'll also need to swab the inside of your mouth to get a DNA sample. We'll use that to rule you out as a suspect. I also need to know if anyone else was in the car or trunk since you bought it."

The owner shoved his hands in the front pockets of his jeans. "I'm a one-man show and no one but me has done so much as sniffed around it since I brought it home from auction." He kicked a rock. "That's the last cop car I'll ever buy. This is number three, and I never made a dime off any of them."

David drove on to Waco to meet with Captain Crow and give him a report of the latest development. No more had he stepped out of his SUV than he stood face to face with Pancho Grimes. The man wore a vest made from a blue jean jacket with a purple heart medal pinned to it. He also had on a sweat-stained camo baseball cap that clearly delineated his participation in actions in the Middle East.

Instead of shaking hands, the man squinted and demanded, "You a Ranger?"

"No. But I remember you from Afghanistan. Your name is Pancho and you're Holly Grimes' uncle."

His squint became more pronounced. "Yeah. I remember you now. Sorry I didn't recognize you. My memory ain't what it should be. Things come and go. You and that tall, pretty lady were at the funeral. I don't recall anyone else from Riverview being there except that nice man named Billy Paul. He and I hit it off real good."

With the sun beating down, David didn't want to continue the conversation standing in the parking lot. "Why don't we find some shade?"

Pancho shook his head. "Can't stay. Got to get home. Trot lines to run."

"I wouldn't mind doing some of that myself. What brings you to Waco?"

"Trying to get a straight answer. Drugs killed the sweetest girl that ever drew a breath. I want to know who did it and what's being done to catch them."

Taking a step forward, David rested his hand on Pancho's shoulder. "It might not look like it, but a lot of good people are working hard to find out who did it. The best thing you can do is go home and keep track of the news."

"The news? They don't know nothin', and Captain Crow won't let me in the building anymore. I have to catch him in the parking lot and then he don't tell me nothin'. Besides that, I don't own a TV, let alone a computer."

A thought came that might give Captain Crow a break and satisfy Pancho. "It just so happens I know Billy Paul. If there's an arrest, I'll have him call you." He paused. "Do you own a phone?"

He pulled a flip phone from his back pocket. "How else could I run a backhoe business without a phone?"

David pulled a pen and small notepad from his pocket and wrote down the phone number.

The wild-eyed veteran removed the hat from his head and shook David's hand. "I appreciate it. You can tell Captain Crow I won't be pestering him no more if Billy Paul calls me once a week."

After seeing Pancho to his truck, David entered the air-conditioned building and stepped toward Captain Crow's office.

"Enter," came the command from his supervisor after David knocked. The Ranger captain looked up from his desk, took off reading glasses, and leaned back. "I hope you have good news."

"What do you want to hear first? Good news concerning Pancho Grimes or possible good news about Amy Sneller's murder?"

"Pancho. That man ambushes me in the parking lot at least three times a week."

David couldn't help but smile. "Billy Paul Stargate has a soft spot for Pancho. I told him Billy Paul would keep him posted on developments."

"That Lonny Martini college kid is already in custody. Isn't that enough for Pancho?"

"We can't prove it was Lonny that sold the moonshine or lollipop that killed Holly. All we have so far is felony possession, delivery, and intent to deliver. I don't think that will satisfy your new best friend."

Captain Crow ran a palm over his chin. "I can't blame Pancho for wanting justice, and I'm not so callus that I don't appreciate the sacrifice he made."

David eased into a chair. "Like I said, Billy Paul has a soft spot for Pancho. I'll ask him to call Pancho once a week.

Even if he doesn't have progress to report, I think it will satisfy him to hear that we're still working to find the person responsible for Holly's death."

"And speaking of. Did you track down a second vehicle?"

"I had to go to the dealership, an auto auction, and a used car lot to find it, but as we speak a Bell County forensics team is tearing apart a black and white Crown Vic. It looked like blood in the trunk."

Gray eyes darted from side to side, as if looking for something to focus on. The captain's head bobbed in a sign of approval. "If there's DNA that matches what was under Amy Sneller's nails, we'll be halfway home. All we'll need to do is find out who the man in the car was."

He looked up. "Have you had lunch yet?"

David shook his head. "What about you?"

The response was a scoffing laugh. "I didn't risk running the gauntlet with Pancho layin' in wait for me. Let's find some ribs and talk about how to proceed if we hit pay dirt with forensics." He paused. "There's something else I've been hearing whispers about that you need to hear. A name bubbled to the top in connection with drugs in the Killeen area."

"Who's that?"

"Tig Murphy."

David's heart skipped a beat. "Big's brother?"

"That's right, and that's why I'm taking you off the task force. There's no shortage of crimes to investigate, and if Tig Murphy is running the show, the press will have a field day with you and CJ."

After swallowing hard, David asked, "When were you planning on telling CJ?"

Captain Crow settled a white straw Stetson on his graying hair. "I was going to call her this afternoon, but after that crack about Pancho being my new best friend, I'll let you handle it. She's your wife. You can tell her whenever you're ready. If it were me, I'd wait until we had more intel."

"That's probably the smart thing to do, but she has a way of finding out things."

"Like I said, she's your wife."

They were walking out the front door as Blake's SUV pulled into a parking spot. Captain Crow pointed at the Ranger who was about to lose his assistant. "You're driving and David's buying. He has a lot to tell you."

CHAPTER NINETEEN

David eased to a stop at a service station on the south side of Waco. Hot wind lifted his hat as soon as he opened the door. He took it off and tossed it on the dashboard. Low clouds scuttling up from the coast carried an untold amount of moisture and energy. Captain Crow warned him the forecast called for severe thunderstorms as the evening progressed. He looked again and saw clouds swirling high above, but they soon drifted apart like nervous teens at a middle school dance.

Still full from ribs and all the trimmings, he decided a fountain drink would suffice for supper. The time on David's phone read 6:17 p.m. With any luck, he'd be home before dark, so no need to call CJ. He still hadn't decided if he was going to tell her about the possibility of Tig Murphy being involved in the drugs in this area. He'd almost talked himself into putting it off until he had more intel from Blake.

The trip through Temple went without incident other than the normal heavy traffic on I-35. Once past the city limit sign, his police radio chattered with reports of high wind and hail. Ever-darkening clouds continued to pass overhead. With each passing mile, he noticed the gray ceiling move lower and thicken. The first report of a tornado came as he passed Belton and the turnoff to Fort Hood. A deputy sheriff reported it, but it was well to the west of the interstate. No reports of damage or injuries.

Distant flashes of lightning came with alarming frequency as he drove south. With no further reports of anything but straight-line winds, small hail, and heavy rain, he passed Salado and the rest areas built for evenings such as this. They had reinforced walls and could withstand a tornado's fury, or so the experts predicted. The parking lots, both for private vehicles and big rigs, were full to overflowing while people moved toward shelter like so many bees returning to their hive.

He'd traveled this road so many times as a state trooper that each overpass and side road was as familiar as his own face in the mirror. If worse came to worst, he'd park under an overpass until the rain and hail passed. It wouldn't be his first time to dodge a thunderstorm.

A couple of miles past the rest stop, the sky turned an unearthly shade of green. He activated his emergency lights, pulled off the interstate, and wove his way around two cars that had the same idea of saving their vehicles under a concrete umbrella. This put him parked on a steep slope, but protected. His door almost got away from him as he opened it and gravity took over.

Once outside, he smelled heat mixed with dry grass and exhaust fumes. The wind calmed. He went to the back of his SUV and pulled out the top half of a waterproof rain suit emblazoned with STATE POLICE and put it on.

The wailing sound of a tornado alert siren reached his ears. Then he saw it. He'd been close to one before, but not this close. It looked to be three-quarters of a mile away when it topped a rise and dropped over a hill, churning everything in its path. Cars and trucks continued to speed by. How could the drivers not see it and stop?

David used the steering wheel to pull himself back into his SUV, put the vehicle in gear and reached for the microphone, all in one continuous motion. Stilling his nerves, he announced his badge number. Dispatch repeated it back.

"Tornado on the ground a quarter mile west of mile marker 279. It's headed east and should cross the interstate." He didn't bother activating his siren. The tornado made noise enough on its own. He gained speed enough to keep cars from crashing into him while straddling two of the three lanes of traffic, then slowed and stopped at an angle. Heat continued to radiate up from the interstate. He stood with his hands up for traffic to stop. A new red F150 pickup had to move against the center guard rail to miss him, but stopped all the same. The driver piled out and ran to him. Before he could speak, David grabbed him by the sleeve of his shirt. "Tell everyone to get in a ditch or low place and cover their heads as best they can."

The man stared at him.

"Go!"

David turned to see a sight out of a science-fiction movie. The tornado raced down the embankment, spread churning destruction onto the interstate, and wobbled as if confused which way to turn. It chose south for ten interminable seconds, changed its mind, then the leading edge leaned to the east again. A red van came from the vortex as if it was a watermelon seed spit by an angry giant. It landed fifty yards in front of David's vehicle.

He was back on the radio with his call sign. "Roll EMS and fire from both directions. Expect multiple causalities." He tried to see through the driving rain and hail, but couldn't.

Dodging a fence post, a dead cow, and many other objects to get to the van, he made it and dreaded what he'd find. The driver's door lay somewhere other than near the mangled vehicle. Hail peppered his head, the icy chunks like cold whacks from a ball peen hammer.

Was it a voice he heard? No. A cry—a child's cry, and it came from the van. Glass covered the interior. The driver's seat sat empty. He gazed into the back and viewed a small, blood-covered face staring back at him. The small mouth was so wide open with shrieks, David could see the back of the throat. He scrambled in through the open door and pushed the red button between pudgy legs. The latch still worked, and he soon held the screaming toddler in his arms as he backed out of the car. He leaned over as he walked back to his vehicle to keep hail from pounding the soft skin of the little one whose cries intensified.

The red pickup pulled up, and the man ran to where David stood. "I can take him. I've had some first aid training and I have one about his age."

"Thanks. I need to check the van to make sure there's no one else in there."

The last thing David heard the child utter was a repeat of, "Mama, Mama, Mama." A check of the van revealed nothing except a woman's purse that lay on the passenger's side floorboard. He retrieved it and took it to his SUV, which by this time had a cracked windshield and hundreds of hail dents.

The hail had moved on and the rain showed some signs of abating. He got back on the radio to give a more thorough report. "I-35 blocked in both directions by overturned semis, multiple vehicles, livestock, and debris. One child found alive with head injury. One woman missing."

He'd been a highway patrol officer for ten years and thought he'd seen every kind of tragedy imaginable, but the destructive ferocity of the tornado was in a class by itself. He knew undiscovered death waited as first responders arrived and searched for more casualties and fatalities.

That was for later. For now, he took in a breath, let it ease out, and opened the purse. He found a wallet and popped open the snap. The woman's photo showed a smiling, brown-haired woman. The card told him her name was Angie South-well. He might someday forget that name, but he'd never forget the other name the child cried out for. "Mama, Mama, Mama."

HEADLIGHTS PIERCED the pre-dawn blackness as CJ gazed out the front window of their home and issued a prayer of thanks for David's return. She stepped into his office and turned off the scanner that had kept her informed of the tragedy. Quiet came when she moved back into the adjoining living room and turned off the local news, still focused on the string of tornadoes that attacked central Texas and were now marching into Louisiana.

The thunderstorm that passed over their farm had been intense, but brief, causing no damage except a few broken limbs. It did, however, cool things enough that she wore a robe over her sleep shorts and one of David's T-shirts. She scurried to the carport and waited. The reason it took David so long to make the trip from the cattle guard to their home became apparent when he pulled under the lights. His SUV looked like someone attacked it with marbles shot from a cannon. The front windshield had a spider web of cracks, as did the windows on the passenger's side.

When he stepped out, her breath caught. Both hands wore bandages, the right more than the left, and his hair lay flat in dried blood. She hooked her hand under his arm and he leaned heavily on her. Without words they moved inside, where she pulled out a chair for him from the table in the breakfast nook. As she knelt, he lifted a boot. "Be careful. There might be glass."

"Is that what happened to your hands?"

His gaze went past her, as if still fixed on what he'd witnessed. "Glass, twisted metal, barbed wire, corrugated tin, nails, you name it."

After pulling off his boots, she moved to the sink, squirted her hands with soap and ran them under warm water. An examination of his head proved futile because of his hair being matted with so much dried blood. "You'll need to shower before I can assess the damage."

He didn't argue. "An EMT checked me over. Everything is superficial, and there was no use trying to get into an emergency room. She suggested I call my GP in the morning and see if I need a tetanus booster."

They both had been through trauma training that taught them to talk freely about what they'd seen and heard in high-stress situations. She recognized his flat affect and not wanting to divulge what he'd seen. Both were classic signs that the very thing he didn't want to do was the thing he needed most. He moaned when she hooked a hand under his arm, lifted, and helped him rise to his feet. With his arm draped over her shoulder, she guided him to their bathroom where she turned on the shower and helped him disrobe. "Don't get in until I get your hands covered."

A quick trip to the kitchen yielded two zip-lock bags and a roll of tape.

Pink water ran down his face, shoulders, and out the drain. "This is going to hurt, but I need to shampoo your head."

He didn't respond other than to nod.

Her fingers moved over welts that felt like bee stings. "Some are bleeding again. I'll put a towel on your pillow tonight." Then she dressed him for bed.

A bathroom cabinet held the next thing David needed. She retrieved three extra strength Tylenol capsules and told him to open his mouth. She popped them in and lifted a water-filled glass to his lips.

Instead of allowing him to lie flat in bed, she put three pillows behind him. "You're going to tell me about it."

He cut his eyes toward her and heaved a sigh.

In a way it seemed cruel to make him relive the experience, but she didn't back down. "You know you need to tell me what happened. We both promised."

His tale started at the gas station south of Waco and didn't end until he crossed the cattle guard to their home. She interrupted from time to time to pull out more details. All went well until he mentioned the van with the missing door. His voice cracked and tears flowed when he spoke of the child calling out for his mama.

Unlike the tornado that had hit with such speed, grief eased away like a receding tide. Details of first responders arriving and performing acts of heroism brought emotional balance. The stories didn't all end in tragedy. Miracles of lives spared outnumbered deaths and serious injuries. Then, unburdened, he yawned and closed his eyes.

She leaned him up and removed two of the pillows, allowing him to slide between the sheets. She did the same.

After waiting a few seconds, she said, "Honey."

"Mmm."

"I'm late."

"Uh-huh, it's late."

His breathing deepened before she could correct him. Turning toward the only man she'd ever loved, she rested her hand on his chest. He didn't respond.

CHAPTER TWENTY

Conversations at the Campus Grind rose to a crescendo, only to fall to a gentle roar. The mid-morning crowd of students and a few brave faculty members came to receive their doses of caffeine and high-carb treats. They either stayed and socialized, or scurried to their next class, or wherever else they had to go. Among those choosing to stay, as usual, was Aunt Bea. An exaggerated wave caught CJ's eye as soon as she entered.

A week had passed since the tornado and she'd only spoken to Bea once, and that wasn't an actual conversation, but a series of text messages. Giving in to temptation, she added a large peanut butter cookie to the coffee order. Bea insisted on a hug when she arrived at her table.

"I see Nancy pretty regular," said Bea. "But how long has it been since my across-the-fence-neighbor came to see me?"

"Too long, and I have big news."

Bea rubbed her hands together like a greedy banker in a black and white movie. She leaned back and tilted her head. "Are you on the nest?"

All the air went out of CJ's surprise balloon. "How did you guess?"

She pointed to the peanut butter cookie. "You're glowing like a firefly, and you never eat peanut butter cookies. If you'd come over with an apple fritter or a raspberry scone, I wouldn't have guessed."

The blue eyes of her confidant caught the light and seemed to shimmer. "What did David say?"

After pinching off a bite of the over-sized cookie, CJ delayed putting it in her mouth. "I haven't told him yet." She popped in the bite, but continued to talk around it. "I wanted to be absolutely sure. That child losing his mother in the tornado hit him hard. It brought back memories of us losing our little girl. Besides, it took over a week after I did the EPT to get an appointment with my OB-GYN. She confirmed it this morning."

"If that doesn't bring a smile to David's face, I don't know what will. How's he doing?"

CJ wiggled her hand to communicate his recovery wasn't complete. "He took a week off and spent it helping his dad, even though he couldn't do much because of the cuts on his hands. They had to replace him from coordinating the big case in Killeen, but that didn't bother him."

"What's the latest on that?"

Something caught CJ's attention on the other side of the room. Peter Starks handed a business card to a young man with Greek letters on his shirt. She turned back to Bea. "He's out of the loop on that one. Someone's stealing miniature horses and he's in charge of the case."

A chuckle bubbled up from Bea. "Are they using a mini-van to haul them in?"

It was CJ's turn to laugh. "I'll ask him tonight." She took another bite of cookie. "Do you know what would make this better?"

"Tell me."

"Peanut butter spread on top of it."

As both women had a friendly laugh, Yari joined them wearing her chef's coat and an apron. "Something funny?"

"We're just enjoying some small talk," said Bea.

Laughter spilled from both women at the table, to the point people stared. CJ placed a hand on Yari's arm. "Don't mind us. David's working on a case that involves people stealing miniature horses, and we were trading jokes."

"I get it," said Yari. "You were horsing around."

Whether she meant to join the fun or not, it didn't matter. Both Bea and CJ laughed until tears came to their eyes.

After the mirth came under control, Yari asked about the quality of the cookie. Bea answered, "You'd better keep these in stock. You're going to have a steady customer."

"Huh?"

CJ leaned toward Yari to whisper a secret. "Keep this under your hat, but I'm going to have a baby and I'm craving peanut butter."

Yari's eyes tried to match the diameter of the cookie. "Cool. When are you due?"

"It will be a Christmas baby."

"Double cool. From now on I'll decorate the peanut butter cookies with red, green, and white stripes. It will be our secret."

CJ noticed a change in the chef's countenance. "Is something wrong?"

Yari nodded. "Can you come to the kitchen, and would you mind using the back entrance? There's something I need to show you, and I don't want it going around that I'm a snitch."

Bea stood. "I need to be running along. Call me tonight, CJ."

After finishing her cookie, CJ rose and walked through a maze of tables to the front entrance. Instead of turning right, she wheeled to the left and followed the hall until she came to an exit. In another minute she took possession of a brown paper bag. Unfolding the top, she saw a water bottle with a half-inch of clear liquid in it.

"A girl that busses tables found this last night. It was on a table with three others that were empty. She said the guys had sodas they poured this stuff in. That's what caught her eye. Why would someone pour water into a cup of soda?"

CJ thanked Yari and left the same way she came in, taking a longer walk back to her office than she intended. She placed her portable radio in its charger and unscrewed the cap off the bottle. It might have been the combination of alcohol fumes mixing with the taste of peanut butter cookies still in her mouth or a touch of morning sickness. Whatever caused it, she gagged.

The radio on her desk came to life with Maria's call sign. She reported being out of her car at the men's athletic dorm parking lot.

Instead of using her radio, CJ pulled out her phone. "Anything exciting?"

"Come to the jock dorm. You'll want to see this."

The radio went back into the pocket of her blazer and she hustled to her vehicle. The trip only took a couple of minutes and at first, nothing looked out of place. Then she followed Maria's pointing finger. The front right side of a Honda accord stood six inches higher than the rest of the car. As she moved around the car, she let out a moan. The driver had parked dead center between the white lines, but on top of a motorcycle.

Maria gave the next bit of information. "The Honda belongs to a freshman that lives in 217. The owner of the

Harley Sportster is a senior. Something tells me he will not be happy about this."

CJ shook her head and was on the verge of going to the freshman's room when Maria said, "There's something else. Look on the passenger's seat."

Two empty, twelve-ounce water bottles lay on the seat along with empty bottles of a sports drink. "It's unlocked," said Maria.

The smell of alcohol and vomit hit CJ the moment she opened the door. If her stomach had done a slow roll after sniffing the bottle in her office, this time it did aerial acrobatics. She slammed the door, ran as far as she could before she stopped, grabbed her knees, and literally lost her cookie.

Maria waited in place until CJ returned. "You've dealt with hundreds of drunks. I didn't expect that to bother you."

Turning into the wind helped. CJ took steps toward her vehicle and said, "I wasn't pregnant when I was arresting drunks."

Maria's eyebrows rose at the new information.

"Find the car's owner, bring him in, and run a Breathalyser before the senior discovers what happened and rips his head off."

The cool air from the air conditioner helped bring her rolling stomach under control. Water bottles filled with moonshine were back on campus. Not what she needed with the end of the semester only weeks away.

FAMILIAR CREAKS CAME from the back-porch swing as CJ tried to come up with a unique way of telling David a special present for Christmas was on the way. Yeah. That might work. She'd get a box, wrap it in festive paper, put bright bows on it and leave it so he'd be sure to find it before they went to bed. She rose and went about searching for the supplies needed to make the surprise memorable.

Her well-laid plans hit a snag when David's replacement SUV approached and she had to scurry to hide a shoe box, scissors, tape, paper, and recycled bows. He'd most likely work in his office later, so she didn't worry about being able to complete the project.

He gave her a quick kiss, made sure nothing was amiss, and walked to his office where he put whatever pistol he carried that day in a gun safe the size of a tall chest-of-drawers. Soon after Nancy moved in last fall, he also purchased two biometric pistol safes that sat on the twin nightstands beside their king-size bed. Both he and CJ were only a touch of their index finger away from having a loaded pistol in their hand. A scanner read their fingerprint and the safe, only big enough to hold a pistol, popped open. Child-safe yet readily accessible, it was one of the best and most sensible purchases they'd ever made.

"Where's Nancy and Davey?" he asked after returning from his office.

She put a finger to her lips to shush him and whispered. "In her room reading books that are mainly pictures. Let's go to the back porch."

"Aren't you hungry?"

"Not much. I had a peanut butter and jelly sandwich when I got home." She grinned and wanted to tell him about her new craving, but didn't want to spoil the surprise. Instead, she tried to look sheepish. "Sorry I didn't wait for you."

"A sandwich is all I want tonight, too, but it will be something a little more substantial than PB&J. I'll get it later. We need to talk."

A flutter of excitement hit her, but she didn't have the

surprise ready yet. "My iced tea is on the back porch. Join me for some swing time."

Their home faced southwest, which guaranteed evening shade and a windbreak from winter's icy claws. Still a couple of hours from dark, they had plenty of time to catch up with each other. She then toyed with the idea of just coming out and telling him her big news.

With an insulated tumbler of tea with ice clinking against the side, David joined her on the swing. "What's the latest on moonshine and drugs on campus?"

She turned to face him. "That's an interesting way to start a conversation."

He shrugged. "Just curious. Would you rather start by telling me about your day?"

She patted his thigh. "Either way, I'll be talking about moonshine." She gave him the details of water bottles with moonshine showing up on campus and a nice motorcycle falling victim to a freshman pole vaulter who parked his car on top of a defensive lineman's two-wheeled pride and joy.

He remained uncharacteristically silent, so she squeezed his thigh. "Your turn. Did you round up some pint-sized ponies?"

A moan came from her right. "If I hear one more pun, or rhyme, or joke about miniature horses, I'm going to buy a water gun and start shooting people."

"It's good-natured ribbing, and you have to admit, it's funny and serious at the same time."

He stared at her. "How would you like to be called 'The Low Ranger'?"

A laugh that sounded like the cackle of a frightened hen burst out. She tried to stop laughing, but a mental image of David riding a horse with his boots dragging the ground stuck in her mind.

"I thought it was funny the first couple of times I heard it. It's the last thirty that got on my nerves."

After a number of back-and-forth trips on the swing, she eventually stopped giggling. He'd been silent for a little too long when he turned to her. "I had a reason for asking about drugs and moonshine on campus. I learned today that an arrest is near in the murder of Amy Sneller. If the search of the suspect's home turns out the way Blake expects, it might put an end to fentanyl-laced lollipops."

The swinging stopped as soon as she heard Amy's name. She turned, but David wouldn't make eye contact with her.

"There's more," he said after a dramatic pause. "Bell County detectives worked an anonymous tip on who might be the ringleader. They collected his garbage from the street and got a DNA sample from saliva on a beer bottle. It matched that taken from a hair found in the trunk of the Crown Vic."

The world seemed to slow down. CJ sat up straight. "Anything else?"

"Two things. The first is, the arrest is going to be made tonight. The second is, the guy's name is Tig Murphy."

Tension gripped every muscle. A nightmarish scene replayed in her mind of a hot summer night and a giant of a man pinning her hands behind her while her state trooper's cowboy hat tumbled to the ground. But that wasn't the most vivid memory. It was the second man, that made her blood run cold again. She saw him take off his belt. Then, the brass buckle came at her face, followed by the sting of flesh ripping from her left ear to the corner of her eye. She smelled again the stale beer on the captor's breath and the stench. Memories of her head crashing into the giant's face weren't clear, nor were the memories of her shaking off his grip, drawing her pistol, and putting two rounds into the chest of the man in front of her.

Once again, her ears rang from the retort as the man facing her drew a chrome-plated pistol and got off a shot that somehow missed her. Repeated practice in drawing and firing had saved her life, but didn't keep her from the memory of an escaped felon promising to violate her and then kill her. She also remembered his name. Bigalou Murphy.

Coming back to herself, she asked a question that she already knew the answer to. "Big's brother?"

"One of them. Sid Murphy is still in prison." David covered her hand with his. "And that's where Tig's going. The case is solid."

The rattle of a vehicle coming down the gravel back road that joined their farm with Bea and Billy Paul's massive ranch reached their ears and both stood. Billy Paul, wearing his customary John Deere baseball hat and overalls, stepped out of the one-ton diesel and walked past the pool. He nodded a greeting. "I need a little help. Doc Lyles is out of town and I've got a heifer that's having trouble with her first calf. My fat hand can't get far enough up her to feel what's going on. I think the calf is breach."

CJ looked at David. "Can you watch Davey?"

"Sure. I take it you're taking Nancy with you?"

"It's been a while since I pulled a calf and those long, skinny arms may be just what we need."

Billy Paul added, "I've got the mama in the barn and she was still standing when I left."

As CJ went to get Nancy, she thought about how often she'd heard the word *mama* in the last two weeks and how she'd get to use it later tonight when she told David. The corners of her mouth pulled up. The imminent capture of Tig Murphy should slow the increasing reports of drugs and moonshine on campus and Alice could start the new chapter of her life without a school scandal putting a blot on her career.

When CJ and Nancy came out with the redhead carrying her veterinary go-bag, David was finishing a conversation with Billy Paul. "I'll call you as soon as I'm sure they have him in custody, and you can call Pancho."

Nancy piled into CJ's farm truck and hollered, "Let's go save a mama and baby."

CHAPTER TWENTY-ONE

CJ slipped into the booth at the Black Skillet diner. "This is a treat. Is there any special reason you're taking me out for breakfast?"

"You deserve it," said David. "Call it an early celebration for making it through another semester."

"There's still another week."

David waved away the difference. "This will put us closer to Lonny Martini's attorney's office. We have an hour to kill before our appointment."

Looking around the down-in-the-heels restaurant, CJ wondered what it was about the place that made it a local institution. The chairs didn't match, and the tables were notoriously wobbly. She used her left hand to scoot over an inch in the booth and felt a seam patched with blue duct tape. Perhaps it was the wait staff that made the place unique. They knew your name, but invariably called everyone hon, sugar, sir, or ma'am, depending on their mood.

She watched Shirley, a brassy woman in her forties, deliver an oval platter of three eggs, four strips of crisp bacon and a stack of hotcakes to a young man scrolling through something on his phone. After plopping the plate in front of him, she placed her hand on his shoulder. "Put that thing away, hon, and enjoy your meal. Whatever you're looking at is likely to give you indigestion."

CJ looked at David and they both chuckled. He leaned toward her, elbows on the table. "Shirley serves advice along with the meal. No extra charge."

The server sashayed to their table and took out an order pad. "I thought you two done moved. How ya' been?"

"Tolerable," said David. "How 'bout you, Shirley?"

"Puttin' one foot in front of the other. My youngest got assigned to an aircraft carrier. She'll be out to sea for Lord knows how long." A sigh came from Shirley, but she didn't stay distracted for long. The sight of a man at the table halfway across the room with his coffee cup raised caught her eye. "I see you, Luther. Be there in a sec."

She leaned over. "He's already had half a pot. More than likely he'll be in the little boy's room before I can get to him."

"I'll take my usual," said David, without being asked what he wanted.

"A short stack with sausage," said CJ. "And could you get me a small bowl of peanut butter on the side?"

Shirley stopped writing. "Sugar, are you nestin'?"

David placed his hands on the table. "If I had a cigar, I'd give it to you."

"And I'd smoke it or chew it after work, depending on how my day went." She looked down at CJ. "When's the stork coming?"

"Right around Christmas."

"All four of mine were summer babies. Nine months after the first good frost." She continued to scribble on her pad. "I'm adding a glass of milk at no charge."

Time seemed to slow down in the diner, almost as if transported back in time to when she was a child and would go to a coffee shop with her father. The nostalgia burned away when David asked, "Do you have your questions ready for Lonny Martini?"

She nodded. "I'm surprised the DA called and said Lonny's lawyer advised him to cooperate."

"Not fully," David reminded her. "He's only willing to talk about moonshine."

"What does that tell you?"

"I guess we'll find out in about forty-five minutes."

She considered David's non-answer and took a stab at responding to her own question. "It tells me there might be a separate moonshine operation here in Riverview County."

David's half smile told her he'd already come to the same conclusion. "That would explain why your officers are finding more and more funny smelling water bottles in the trash at the dorms."

"They hated it when we went through the trash last week, but it gave us a good idea of how many underage drinkers we have. John and Alice think it's a fad, but I'm not so sure."

CJ placed her hand over her stomach, something she'd done more and more since the EPT read positive. Her thoughts shifted back to moonshine. "I never thought Central Texas would be a good place for brewing moonshine."

"Why not?"

"We have lousy water. It comes from lakes and reservoirs and has so many minerals and chemicals it tastes like chlorine and limestone."

"Not all water. Go deep and you'll find the good stuff."

"That must be why the water on the farm I grew up on tasted good. Daddy said we had a deep well that went all the way down to the aquifer."

Shirley returned carrying a platter in her hand, a second plate on her wrist, and a coffee pot in her right hand. "I'll be right back with your milk, sugar."

David smiled down on his omelet, biscuits, and sausage gravy.

The meal progressed with no more talk about moonshine, Lonny Martini, or Tig Murphy. They finished their meal and made it to the attorney's office with time to spare.

Their destination, a law office, was a block away from the county courthouse, housed in a building built when reins were strung through embedded rings in the concrete sidewalks to tether horses. The rock building had been home to many businesses, including the local newspaper. The latest transformation occurred many years ago when a video game rental store became a law office. All it took was a good imagination, a skilled contractor, and plenty of money.

It proved to be a one-man, two-woman operation. Husband and wife attorneys shared a receptionist with amazing keyboard speed. They had ten minutes to witness the middle-aged woman's proficiency. She was one of those people who didn't move a muscle that didn't go into completing a task.

As if notified by telepathy, she looked up from her computer monitor. "Mr. Rhinehart is ready to see you." She shifted only her eyes to a hallway. "Third door on your right."

The attorney rose to greet them, but Lonny remained seated and silent. CJ acknowledged his presence with a nod. His head dipped, a classic sign of shame.

"Please have a seat," said Mr. Rhinehart as his hand showed two chairs on the opposite side of a conference table. "I want to go over the basics of the agreement the district attorney and I came to before you ask my client questions."

David and CJ both nodded.

"Mr. Martini has agreed to answer questions related to his participation in the sale and delivery of alcohol and marijuana to students of Agape Christian University. I'm still in negotiations with the DA on other charges, and I've advised my client not to respond if you swerve off the narrow path."

David sat silent because they'd agreed CJ would do most of the questioning. "We understand the agreement. I also understand this conversation is to be recorded."

David pulled his phone from his pocket and manipulated it to record. He gave the proper preamble, identified all the participants, confirmed that the statements made were voluntary, and that Lonny had the right to discontinue the interview if he chose to.

CJ began. "How long have you been selling marijuana to ACU students, Mr. Martini?"

Lonny's long sleeve shirt looked wrinkled, but clean, and he'd shaved the stubble from his face. "Three years."

"Were you working under Amy's direction?"

"Yes."

"Tell us in your own words how you came to be involved in selling marijuana."

What followed was a tale of sporadic use in high school until his senior year when he picked up extra cash for selling to a few select friends he trusted. This morphed into a similar pattern in college, until Amy approached him to sell for her as he was going into his junior year.

David asked, "How could you be sure the people you were selling to were college students?"

The attorney held up his hand for Lonny not to answer.

"It's all right, Mr. Rhinehart." He looked at David and then CJ. "She had a system to make sure. Before we could sell to anyone, we had to give their name to Amy. She'd check it against the current student directory. If enrolled, we'd fill the order. If not, we'd tell them to get it someplace else."

The meeting progressed with one minor detail following another. Lonny didn't know for a long time how many other dealers Amy had recruited. That changed a year ago when she selected him as the heir-apparent to the business, and they moved in together. The true scope of her business came when Lonny said, "Until I got busted, there were six sellers. She limited how many students could sell, and we were on a sliding scale. The more Amy trusted them, the more customers they could have." He summarized. "She designed the business to not get so big it drew attention. She had her sales goals and met them, and that was plenty for her and us sellers."

"Are you sure it was enough for you?" asked David.

Lonny's head dipped and his voice came out weak and contrite. "I was stupid and wanted more."

"Is that when you started selling moonshine?" asked CJ.

He nodded.

"You need to respond verbally."

"Yes."

"What are the names of the students that sold for Amy?"

The attorney spoke up. "That information isn't part of the agreement and it won't do you any good, even if it was. Mr. Martini will explain."

"When Amy was murdered, every one of our sellers told me they were through. They meant it and they lost their source when she died because Amy handled that herself. You'd be wasting your time in going after them. They'll all deny any involvement in selling pot and there's no evidence."

CJ still hadn't tied Amy or Lonny to their source. "Where did the pot come from?"

"Amy never told me. She said that would be the last thing I'd learn from her, and it would only come after she had her master's and was out of Texas."

"Back to the moonshine," said CJ. "When did you first hear about it coming on campus?"

She could tell the attorney had prepared Lonny well by his

sure answer. "Right before spring break, when the Grimes girl died. Even then, all I heard was through the grapevine."

The memory of the hospital and the parents' grief once more hit CJ hard. David must have sensed it and took over. "You didn't sell it to her?"

"No." The answer came quick and sure.

"When did you first sell moonshine to campus students?"

"Right after Amy disappeared."

"Where did it come from?"

"I didn't ask. I assumed it was left-over stock from South Padre Island."

CJ was ready to get back in the game. "Sergeant Vasquez took photos and video of you receiving moonshine from a man driving a blue Sonata. Did you know the man?"

His pony tail went side to side as he shook his head. "Never met him before or since."

"Would it surprise you to hear they arrested him in connection with drugs, including fentanyl?"

The attorney interrupted. "Don't answer that." He looked at CJ. "I'll not tolerate any attempt to link my client to crimes other than the ones referred to at the onset of this interview."

David took over before she said something she might regret, and spoke in a relaxed tone. "What gave you the idea of selling moonshine to ACU students?"

"A guy recruited me."

"Who?"

"A student that moved here last fall from North Carolina."

"Does this student have a name?"

A pause followed where Lonny looked at his attorney and received a nod to proceed. "Peter Starks."

David finished the interview as CJ went through the motions of thanking both the attorney and Lonny for cooperating. A reduced prison sentence and the possibility of probation might be his reward for telling what he knew. He had said nothing about Tig Murphy and next to nothing about his henchman. Not a poor trade, all things considered.

Once in David's vehicle, she pulled out her phone and typed a text to Maria.

Full background on Peter Starks.

Her response came back.

I never trusted him.

One more memory came to her mind, and she gave voice to it. "I saw Peter Starks talking to Randy one day at the Campus Grind. Do you think we need to warn him to stay away from Peter?"

"Not a bad idea. Randy would probably like to hear it from you that there's a baby on the way, too. Let's go see him this evening when it cools off a little."

CHAPTER TWENTY-TWO

David moved to the refrigerator and opened the door to see if leftovers might be fair game for supper. "I caught a break with the miniature horse thieves."

Nancy emitted a pitch-perfect imitation of a whinny as she moved to the table in the breakfast nook, her usual place for evening study.

He closed the refrigerator door harder than necessary. "Half the comedians in the world are unemployed and you're making jokes?"

"No need to get on your high-horse." Nancy flashed a smile.

He looked at CJ, hoping to get in a preemptive strike. "Don't you start in on me too. I've had it up to here with short jokes." His hand slashed across his forehead.

CJ held up her hands, but threw her voice to mock that of an actor in an old TV western. "I come in peace, Low Ranger."

"Just for that, I'm not telling you two what happened."

"Fine with me," said Nancy. "I'm not that fond of short stories."

"Come on honey," said CJ. "Tell us about catching the bad guys."

David shook his finger at her. "Alright, but no more short jokes."

CJ crossed her heart with her finger. "I promise."

"It didn't involve any great skill. It was really just dumb luck. A deputy sheriff made a routine traffic stop on one of the smallest U-Haul trucks they rent. You know the one I'm talking about. It's a pickup truck with a box on the back with extra storage over the cab. They must have sold it at auction because the U-Haul lettering was painted over."

"Why did the deputy pull them over?" asked Nancy.

"Liquid was coming out the back."

"Water?"

"It was water when the horse drank it. Of course, the deputy didn't know where it was coming from. As he walked to the driver's window, one horse kicked the metal side. From all the racket, the deputy thought the driver was into human smuggling. He called for backup and waited until they arrived. It surprised everyone when they rolled up the back door and saw the rear ends of two little horses."

He had to wait until both women stopped snickering. "The driver consented to a search of his farm and we recovered eight more horses. The thief was a strange little guy and swore he didn't take them to sell. Said he always wanted a miniature horse when he was a kid, but his parents wouldn't let him have one. Then, he got married and his wife said no. She left him three months ago and he started collecting."

Nancy shook her head. "People are weird. Were the horses in good condition?"

"They looked good to me. I left the property when the vet arrived." David paused. "The best thing about the deputy solving the crime is he's getting the short jokes I've been hearing ever since Captain Crow dumped it in my lap."

CJ's eyes shifted to look outside. "Let's get to Randy's before it gets dark."

"Tell him I said hi," said Nancy as she opened the screen to her laptop.

David grabbed an apple from a bowl on the counter on his way out.

"That's better sliced with peanut butter on it," said CJ.

"These days you think everything is better with peanut butter on it."

It only took him from the back door to crossing the cattle guard to finish the apple. He lowered his window and threw the core into the pasture. "Feeding the ants."

As he turned onto the blacktop he asked, "Did Maria do the research on Peter Starks?"

He could see CJ nod out of the corner of his eye.

"He's a bit of a paradox. Grew up in Weaverville, North Carolina, a small town close to the Tennessee border."

"That sounds like moonshine country."

"It is. Plenty of wild, hilly country and clean mountain water." She took a breath. "He was valedictorian of his high school class and won a free ride to the University of North Carolina in Asheville. Great grades there, too."

"Any criminal history?"

"Nothing, but he also doesn't have a job history. He's old school and pays for everything he can with cash."

David turned onto another county road. "That's odd. Why did he pick ACU?"

"I've been wondering that. John thinks it's because of the quality education. He's pursuing a double major in chemistry and business management."

"What do you think?"

"The school has a great reputation, but there's more to it than that. I think he came here because there's no competition for selling moonshine, and most of the students are from well-to-do families. Money isn't their problem to getting something illegal to drink; age and access are. Him talking to Amy tells me he was trying to access her organization of sellers. I bet they would have jumped at the chance to sell clear liquid in water bottles instead of baggies of pot."

A mile later, David voiced a thought that added another layer to what CJ theorized. "Tig Murphy must have found out about the pot and moonshine at ACU. He wanted to add hard stuff to the menu. Amy wouldn't play ball, so he eliminated her."

"That's possible," said CJ. "What's the latest on Tig?"

David had to slow for a rabbit to decide which field to dart into before he answered. "His team of lawyers filed a petition for a speedy trial with the judge assigned to hear the case."

CJ turned to face him. "Why would they do that?"

"I spoke with Blake today. He and Captain Crow discussed it, and they believe it's a ploy to get all the evidence revealed in discovery as soon as possible. Then they'll petition the judge for postponements."

Turning in her seat, CJ said, "What do you think?"

He tapped on the steering wheel. "I think the judge made a mistake by granting bail to Tig, even if it was three million dollars. If they end up delaying the trial, that's more time for witnesses to disappear and memories to fade."

CJ pointed. "There's the trailer and the barn, on the right. It looks like he has a new gate."

They turned into the drive to the property but had to stop at the shiny new aluminum gate. David stared at a large sign, warning trespassers to stay out. "New gate, new sign, new chrome chain and a big padlock."

"They weren't here the last time I was here," said CJ. "He must have started his business of working on cars and doesn't want to make it easy for someone to steal his tools or customer's rides."

David unlatched his seat belt. "The only vehicle I see is his car parked by the trailer." He scanned the property. "I can't see any improvements in this place. I thought Randy was more industrious."

CJ shrugged. "He's like most eighteen-year-olds and works at what interests him."

"Give him a call to find out if he's here. He might have left with one of his friends."

On the fifth ring, a response came in a rush over the phone's tiny speaker. "Yeah. I got it plugged."

"Randy?" asked CJ.

"Oh... sorry. I thought it was someone else."

"I'm at the gate. I need to talk to you."

"Uh, stay there. I'll be right up."

Instead of the door to Randy's home swinging open, the afternoon light caught a glint from a door on the barn. David turned to see Randy wiping his hands on a rag and walking with long strides up a gentle slope. He shoved the rag in his back pocket on his way to the gate. Even though the sun had crept below the horizon, there was still enough light to see Randy's shirt was wet with perspiration.

CJ wiped her damp hand on her jeans. "Why don't you open the doors and let some breeze in?"

Randy's gaze didn't meet hers. "I guess I got so into what I was doing, it didn't occur to me." Without taking a breath he asked, "What do you want?"

David bristled. "A more cordial tone of voice would be a good start."

Randy's gaze diverted back to the barn. "Sorry. That didn't come out right. It's been a long day."

"That's all right," said CJ. "I've been a little snippy myself lately. I guess it's because my body's changing."

Randy didn't respond but glanced back to the barn again.

David and CJ traded looks that communicated they didn't know why Randy was acting strange. CJ pressed on. "We came for two reasons. The first is to tell you we're expecting a baby."

"Uh-huh," was his only response.

"The second," said David in a firm tone, "is to tell you to watch out for Peter Starks."

Randy's head jerked around. "Peter Starks? I don't know him."

The lie couldn't have been more obvious if Randy had a neon sign hanging over his head with *LIAR* in bright white letters and an arrow pointed downward.

"We need to come in and talk to you about your relationship with Peter," said CJ.

His unruly head of black hair shook. "I can't let you in."

"Why not?" asked CJ. "I thought we were still on good terms. All we want to do is tell you some things about Peter that you need to know. He's not what he seems, and we don't want you to get in trouble."

A hissing sound came from the barn, followed by an explosion that blew the doors of the barn open and put a hole in the metal roof. Smoke rose and fire licked its tongue through the new hole.

"Call it in, CJ," shouted David. He put a foot on a metal cross-beam, grabbed the top of the gate and launched himself over. Once on the other side, he moved into Randy's personal space. "Give me the keys to the lock."

"I'm not supposed to," he stammered.

"Quit being stupid. Fire trucks are on the way. Do you think a chain and padlock is going to keep them out?"

Randy dug in the front pocket of his jeans and handed over a set of keys. "It's the new shiny one."

David pointed to a dwarf tree halfway to the single-wide.

"Stand by that tree and don't even think about going in the trailer or getting in your car."

The lock clicked open and the gate swung wide. CJ pulled through the opening and drove to where Randy stood. David jogged after her. By the time he arrived, Randy had slumped to the ground and was sitting cross-legged, making circles in the dirt with a stick. He looked at CJ. "How much trouble am I in?"

"Plenty," said David. "And we can't get you out of this one."

"Am I going to prison?"

"You should."

David looked at CJ, wanting to see how she would react.

Her voice lowered, sounding controlled, but firm. "We don't know what's going to happen to you. Manufacturing moonshine is new ground for me, let alone when the still blows up."

David took three steps, turned and walked back. "We interviewed a man this morning who's facing time for delivering moonshine and drugs. He hired an expensive lawyer who advised him to cooperate with the police. That's free advice, but what do I know?"

"Are you going to arrest me?"

"We could," said David. "Either of us, but I think I'll leave that pleasure to the sheriff's department. I hear the sirens. They'll be here shortly."

Randy's nod was one of acceptance of his fate, whatever that might be. He looked at CJ and said, "I'm sorry."

She reached down and rested a hand on his shoulder. "It may seem like the end of the world, but it's not. It's going to take time, but you'll get past this."

The eighteen-year-old swallowed hard and hung his head. CJ's kind words had their effect on Randy, but they also put David on a more even keel. "Stand up. I changed my mind.

You're under arrest. Get in the back seat and don't say anything to anyone except CJ. Not even me. She needs to find out what you know about Peter Starks. What you tell her can't be used against you in court because I'm going to wait to read your rights later."

His dark eyebrows pressed together. "I don't understand. Are you still trying to help me?"

CJ hooked a hand under his arm and guided Randy to his feet. "It's more like damage control, but yes. David's still trying to help you. Now, help yourself and do what he says."

Mixed emotions flooded into David as he watched CJ open the rear door and Randy climb in. Instead of getting in with him, she returned and looked up. "You're a good man, David Harper."

"I'm not so sure. Find out how deep he is into this. We'll talk about what we can do for him after we finish here."

THE FIRST FIRE truck arrived as CJ climbed into the driver's seat. The air conditioner was already blowing and coolness contrasted not only with the sticky evening air but also with the sight of flames coming from the barn. She looked in the rear-view mirror. "Move to the other side of the seat so I can see you."

Randy complied. His shoulders rounded forward, and his gaze didn't rise to view the scene.

"What's that junk all over your jeans?" she asked.

"Oatmeal paste. The still has seams that have to be plugged every time you cook a batch. Otherwise, you lose your steam before it cools, and that's where the liquor is. A paste made of oatmeal and water is how to seal a seam. I thought I had the leak stopped, but then you called and..."

His voice trailed off, but then came back strong enough to

hear. "Peter told me it could blow up, but I didn't think it'd go up like that."

"Did Peter supply you with the still?"

"According to him, I had the perfect setup, and he told me how much money I could make. He said all I had to do was brew it. He'd take care of supplying everything I needed and picking up the finished product. All I had to provide was the water."

So far, so good. Randy's involvement wasn't as deep as she'd first thought. Without her asking, Randy continued. "He gave me a recipe and watched as I mixed the ingredients for the first batch of mash. The temperature in the barn was good for it to ferment. It took several days for it to stop bubbling. He came back, and we cooked off a batch."

"Did he take it with him?"

Randy shook his head. "Peter told me the only time he ever touches moonshine is when he teaches someone to make it. He left all the plastic bottles here and said someone would come by after I finished this batch."

"Did Peter tell you the name of the person coming or how to get in touch?"

A second fire truck and a sheriff's department pickup came through the gate and pulled between the trailer and the barn. Randy brought his gaze back to CJ. "All communication with Peter is one way. He told me to never call him unless it's an absolute emergency. Even then, he won't answer. Everything goes to voice mail."

"Do you have the number?"

He dug in his back pocket and pulled out his wallet. A business card came forward. It was identical to the one Peter gave her when he came to her office. The term *plausible deniability* came to her mind. When confronted, Peter would deny any involvement in moonshine and state he was perfecting his sales skills, like he did every week with plenty of witnesses watching.

Randy's voice sounded small when he next spoke. "I wish I could tell you more about Peter, but I can't. He wore gloves the whole time he was here and even made me leave my phone in the living room while we went to the barn."

"Where did he park?"

"He insisted on parking in the barn."

"Did he buy the new gate, lock and chain?"

"He bought everything... well, sort of. Paying him back would come from what I produced."

"Let me get this straight," said CJ as her temper came to life. "Peter provided a still, bottles, propane, all the ingredients except water, extra security measures for your property, and then puts you on a plan to pay off everything. Is that right?"

"That's not the way he explained it," said Randy with a touch of defense in his voice.

Her voice raised. "What did he tell you everything would cost?"

"Uhh... Uhh."

"That's what I thought. He played you. You fell for the line of a slick salesman and now you're the one going to jail."

His head dipped again. "I'm sorry."

"You already said that."

Two more county patrol cars arrived. David met them and pointed to the gate, the barn, and to his vehicle. It wouldn't be long before they left the scene on their way to check Randy into county jail. She needed to talk to David where Randy couldn't hear them, but first she needed to follow proper procedures. She opened the door and went around the vehicle until she reached the door closest to Randy.

"Get out," she said after she opened the door. "Put your hands on the vehicle and step back. I'm going to search you and then I'm going to handcuff you. Do you have anything in your pockets I need to know about?"

He shook his head and complied. As she ran her hands over his shoulders, she said. "If you have anything illegal on you, tell me now. Believe me, they'll search every inch of you at jail and if they find anything illegal, that's another felony."

"I'm clean. Wait. Pocket knife in left front pocket."

"Don't reach for it. I'll get it."

She knew David had something up his sleeve, but she didn't know what. Whatever it was, they needed to put on a good show. It wouldn't hurt Randy if he thought he was in more trouble than he really was. No one had died or was injured in the explosion. Moonshine from this still never made it outside the barn. Randy didn't have a criminal record, even though he should. A good lawyer would make sure the dispensing of justice would come as a small serving, if at all.

With handcuffs secured, she made her way to David. He excused himself from the deputies and met her. "Get what you needed?"

"Everything he produced is burning up in the barn."

"What about Peter Starks?"

"He found a gullible young man and sold him on a get-rich-quick scheme. Starks' college career at ACU and his moonshine days are nearing an abrupt end."

"Good." David ran his fingers through his hair and gazed at the ever-darkening eastern sky. "Give Billy Paul a call. Tell him what's happened and ask him to hire an attorney for Randy. I'll pay him back." His next words came out in a whisper. "Randy's had it tough, but this is the end of the road for helping him. Agreed?"

"I agree. Let's get him to jail."

CHAPTER TWENTY-THREE

Armed with a large cup of coffee, CJ trudged up the steps of ACU's administration building, took the elevator to the fourth floor, and walked down the hall to Alice's corner office. Normally she'd take the stairs all the way, but she was already perspiring from the walk from her office. Alice's personal assistant didn't bother to look up. "President Cummings and Chief Sylvester are expecting you. Go on in."

As soon as the thick wooden door closed, John motioned CJ to join him and Alice at the conference table. Before them lay three file folders.

"Sorry I'm late," said CJ.

Alice waved away the apology. "We were digesting your report from last night's activities. You and David certainly have a knack for being at the right place at the right time. It appears you nipped Randy's criminal career in the bud."

"We hope so. David's contacting federal agents to see if they want to get involved in prosecution."

"Let's hope not," said Alice. "I've been around Randy long enough to know he has exceptional drive and talent. Perhaps not in the university setting, but he's certainly skilled with car repairs and restorations."

As usual, Alice looked the picture of dignified refinement in a spring outfit of pastels. A few lines of worry, however, creased her brow. She folded her hands as if to pray and took in a deep breath. "I need your help. Both of you."

John straightened his posture. "Of course. What can we do?"

Alice's hands shifted to lie flat on the table. "John, from your reports, I've gleaned that illegal moonshine is being sold to our students, and the problem is increasing. CJ's report from last night's interview with Randy shows we know the identity of the student who's responsible."

John looked down. "Randy helped us by divulging so much."

Alice cast an intense gaze at John. "What I'm about to tell you is not for public consumption. At least not yet." She paused, seemed to search for words, and took a sip from her cup of hot tea.

She settled the cup on the table and began. "You deserve a full explanation. As you're both aware, there's a group of regents who believe the university needs fresh leadership. It's come to my attention that this group is gathering information about me they plan to use in the next board meeting to force me to resign. In fact, they canceled last month's meeting to give themselves time to bolster their case."

John opened his mouth to speak, but she held up her hand. "Let me finish." She took another sip of tea. "Although I may not agree with their tactics or conclusions about my ability to serve, I count it as providential that there's a three-way power split. To be blunt, they don't have the votes to force me out." The beginnings of a smile moved a corner of her mouth.

"It's also possible that I may have the opportunity of a

lifetime to serve as a state representative. If offered, I plan to take it." She took a breath. "John, you should also know that I married Bob over spring break."

John gasped, but then smiled. "That's wonderful." He paused. "I didn't mean that your leaving is wonderful. It's terrible." He got more tongue-tied as he went on. "I mean, it's terrible that they're trying to force you out when you've been so good for the university."

Alice looked at CJ and then back at John. "CJ and David already know the details and why I want to keep my marriage a secret until after I'm accused of moral turpitude. The jackals need to learn a lesson on making accusations without having all the facts. They won't force me out," said Alice with steel in her words. "At least they won't be able to if the university doesn't have a scandal."

John was nobody's fool. "Am I sensing Peter Starks needs to find another university that better suits him?"

"Precisely," said Alice. "And I don't want to know how you do it, but a quiet departure would be best for the university."

CJ and John exchanged conspiratorial glances. "Leave it to us," said John.

As she and John walked across campus, CJ's mind raced. One thought crowded out the next and she verbalized it. "Peter's not only book smart, he's mountain smart. He's dodged getting in trouble for a long time. He's also used to trading and making deals. We have to convince him he wins by leaving."

"I don't understand," said John.

"He'll be willing to leave and we won't have to arrest him if we play this right. I have an idea I want to run by David. First, we need to check on final exams."

"Huh?"

"I'll explain when we get to the office."

THE PHONE CALL from CJ brought a different wrinkle to David's day. His new stepmother needed to get rid of a problem student, and she'd given CJ and John carte blanche on how to do it. It couldn't happen through illegal means, but that didn't mean they couldn't go right to the line and perhaps hang a toe or two over the edge. This could be fun.

He arrived at the university police department at 1:30 p.m. and went directly to CJ's office. John and CJ were there waiting for him. John's eyes danced with excitement. CJ appeared calm, but glowed all the same. Was it anticipation of turning the tables on a student who thought he had the world by the tail, or the beauty that comes with becoming a mother? Perhaps both.

"Tell me how you want to play this," said David.

"I'll let CJ explain," said John.

This didn't surprise David. John, the scholar, didn't take too many opportunities to interview suspects or make arrests. His job was to handle the mountain of paperwork and mesh the goals of the university with the laws of the state. He also taught classes half-time. It was a balancing act which suited him, the small police department, and the university well. Still, John's excitement about being involved in Peter's interview had him wound up.

CJ was the hands-on supervisor and the full-time *de facto* leader of the department. She trained the officers, interacted with them in the field, and doled out either encouragement or discipline. The university policy called for the police chief to have an advanced degree. CJ's BA in criminal justice didn't measure up, thus leading to the unconventional, yet workable, departmental structure.

CJ placed her hand on David's arm. "I'm the good cop

today. You're the bad cop and John is the one who will come in bringing us more information."

"This sounds like a play," said David. "Where's the script?"

"Ad-lib it," said CJ. "Your job is to scare him into leaving. I'm to balance you out and John will pile on reasons he should hit the road."

David looked around her office. "Are we doing the interview in here?"

"In the interview room," said John. "I'll be watching through the one-way mirror and listening. That way I'll know when to come in."

David looked at John. "Don't act surprised if I'm not totally honest about some things I'm going to tell Peter."

John grinned. "I'm familiar with the Supreme Court's decision in Frazier v. Cupp that affirmed police can use certain deceptive practices in interviews. I may stretch the truth myself."

"When will Peter be here?" asked David.

CJ rose and patted David on the arm as she walked by. "Maria's walking him over now. Give me a few minutes alone with him before you come in."

Maria arrived, motioned for Peter to go in the interview room, stepped out, and closed the door. David and John watched through the one-way mirror. Maria joined them. "I wish I could talk to him. I'd have him singing like a little birdie."

As the trio watched, CJ began. "Thanks for coming in, and sorry about the accommodations. They're running new cable to my office. You know how that goes. They can stretch a thirty-minute job into an all-day affair."

Peter gave a furtive glance at the closed door. "I don't mean to be rude about this, but I'm pretty busy. Finals are this week and I need to cram."

She motioned him to have a seat. As expected, he put on

a salesman's smile and eased down. "I wish I could tell you what this is about. We received a call from the Texas Rangers this morning. They're sending one of their investigators to talk to you. I can't imagine why."

CJ looked up from examining her fingernails. "Did you know they selected me to be a Ranger?"

"I heard something about it."

"Yeah. I didn't think I fit in with their culture."

His head tilted. "What do you mean?"

"I'm sure you've heard stories about them. You know, 'One riot. One ranger.' That sort of thing."

"Yeah, I heard it, but I didn't believe it."

She brushed away a non-existent fleck of something from the table. "It probably wasn't true, but it highlights something that is. They're the most tenacious people in law enforcement I've ever seen. They're expected to get results and they don't stop until someone goes to jail. Plenty of stories go around, some complimentary and others, not so much. I hear they're not always careful about following proper procedures, and that round badge on their chest has a way of impressing judges and juries."

This was David's cue to enter. He left the soundproof room, went next door, and slammed the door shut.

He moved his chair out of the way, put his palms flat in the middle of the table, leaned over, and came within a foot of Peter's nose. "A still blew up in this county last night. Start talking."

The directness caused Peter to flinch, but he soon regained his composure. "You must have me confused with someone else. I don't drink alcohol or handle it."

David made a big production of retrieving his chair, sitting down, and leaning back, all without blinking while he stared at Peter. "Is your name Peter Starks?"

"Yes."

"I tell you what, Peter Starks, for every lie you tell me, it will cost you a year in prison, and don't think for a minute that I can't make it happen. Try again. What do you know about a still exploding last night?"

"I heard about it, that's all. I swear."

"Where did you grow up?"

"North Carolina."

David pointed a finger at him. "Where in North Carolina?"

"A small town north of Asheville."

"Moonshine country. You come from the mountains where there're illegal stills in every other holler. It's easy to buy moonshine if you know the right people. Right?"

"They say it is, but—"

"It would also be easy for an enterprising young man to load up a truck with moonshine, come to Texas, and sell it at a popular beach over spring break, wouldn't it?"

David let the question hang in the air for several seconds. Then he lowered the volume and the speed of his words. "Folks around here don't know how to make moonshine. They need someone like you to come in and teach them." He had to admit, Peter was cool under pressure. Most people would have tiny beads of sweat on their top lip by now. Not Peter. Time to turn up the heat.

"Holly Grimes," said David. "You ever hear that name?"

Peter ran a palm over his chin. "The name's familiar. Wasn't she the girl that died of an overdose before spring break?"

David issued a silent nod. "She was drinking moonshine with three other girls in their dorm on the night she died." He didn't wait for Peter to respond. "There's someone in her family that wants to see everyone associated with her death six feet under. I know the man and he's serious."

David launched right into the next attack. "What about Amy Sneller? You were talking to her in the campus coffee shop."

"So? I talk to a lot of people there. Ask anyone." He turned to CJ. "Ask her, she'll tell you."

CJ nodded. "He talks to lots of people. He's losing his fear of rejection by talking to people he has nothing in common with."

David issued an icy stare. "You might like our state prison. They serve a very diverse clientele. I'm sure they'll accommodate you in finding a cell mate you have nothing in common with."

Before Peter could respond, John opened the door. "I have preliminary results from the explosion at Randy McNutt's barn last night. They got a partial cast of tire prints from a car someone parked in the barn. Randy wouldn't tell us who it was, but they're working on matching it to a vehicle."

CJ shook her head. "Even if we get a match, all it will do is narrow the suspect list."

David tilted his head. "It might be a good idea if I checked the tires on your car, Peter." He looked at John. "Anything else?"

"Yeah. Here's a copy of a business card found in Randy's wallet."

David took it, issued a crooked smile, and displayed it so Peter could see it. "You told me you didn't know Randy McNutt. Why was your business card in his wallet?"

Peter's arms crossed over his chest. "I didn't say I didn't know him. I said—"

He didn't get the next sentence out before David interrupted him in a no-nonsense loud voice. "Then you do know him. Good. That's one thing settled."

"Wait, you don't understand."

David lowered his voice and gave him one of his best stares. "No, son. I understand. I understand you're responsible for a lot of bad things at South Padre Island, here in Riverview County, and in Bell County. Let's talk more about Amy Sneller."

Peter leaned forward as if his stomach was bothering him. "You've got to believe me, I only talked to her once."

David looked at John. "I'm hearing a lot of coincidences. Amy Sneller only talked to Peter once, and now she's dead. Holly Grimes had water bottles of moonshine in her dorm room, and she's dead. Randy McNutt talked to Peter once and he had a still blow up. Peter knows about building stills and making moonshine. I'm seeing a pattern of moonshine, death, and people talking to Peter."

David directed his gaze back to the face that didn't look so confident. "You talked to Randy more than once, didn't you?"

"I might have," said Peter. "Like I said. I talk to lots of people."

CJ came to his rescue. "That's what he told me when I asked about the conversations in the Campus Grind."

Peter squared his shoulders, his confidence returning. David didn't mind. The purpose of the interview wasn't to get a full confession, only to give Peter enough reasons to get out of the state and never come back. CJ seeming to be on his side helped to not press him so hard he'd demand an attorney.

David looked at CJ. "I understand Randy told you last night that Peter taught him how to set up the still."

"Well, yeah, but he might have been trying to find someone to share the blame."

"He's lying," said Peter. "He's a hick kid. A loser. I wouldn't waste my time on him."

David leaned back again, trying to look relaxed and smug. "Do you know the biggest problem in being a criminal?"

Peter didn't respond, but that didn't matter. David was going to tell him anyway.

"There's no honor among thieves. I send people to prison all the time based on the testimony of only one person. Sometimes it doesn't matter if it's true or not. People make deals to save their own sorry hides."

David straightened slightly. "Do you know what I see when I look at you?"

Again, he didn't answer, and again, it didn't matter. It was CJ's turn to speak. She looked into Peter's face and spoke in a sympathetic tone.

"I see a young man with an incredible future ahead of him. He grew up poor, but he has a sharp mind and more ambition than I've seen in a long time."

David interrupted. "I see a kid with all kinds of contacts back in the hills of North Carolina. He took a chance, made a huge investment, and took a load of moonshine to a beach during spring break. It paid off, and he came back with more money than he'd ever seen before. So much that he bought himself a Rolex watch. He wanted to keep making money but ran into trouble. Things weren't like they were back in the hills of North Carolina. It was hard to find good water and people he could trust. He tried to buy out a small-time marijuana dealer, but she turned him down. Then, other people came to him, but they scared him to death. They wanted him to deal in hard drugs and help them set up stills all over Central Texas."

CJ shifted her gaze to David and then to John. "If what you say is true, I guess there's nothing left to do but arrest him."

Peter's Adam's apple bobbed. The words hit home.

It was John's turn. "There might be a way out of this. Let me check on something."

"I need a break," said David.

The room cleared of all but CJ and Peter. After a few minutes, she left him alone.

All three and Maria were looking through the glass, watching Peter with hands clasped together in front of him. John spoke first. "I didn't hear all you said to him. Did you continue to bait the hook?"

"I told him the truth," said CJ. "He's smart enough to make piles of money legally. He doesn't need to be involved in moonshine."

"How long should we give him?"

"Long enough for me to go to the little girl's room."

As soon as CJ returned, the trio went to the interview room and sat facing the student who displayed none of his previous confidence.

"Chief Sylvester spoke with your professors," said CJ. "Because of your excellent grades, you're exempt from all finals."

John took over. "Your semester is over and so is your career at ACU. You have two choices. You can pack your car and leave the state today with a clean academic and criminal record, or—"

David broke in. "You'll experience the full weight of the criminal justice system come down on you. Believe me, the State of Texas weighs more than you can bear."

Peter looked into each face and must have decided a change of climate suited him. He stood. "If I'm free to go, I'll do just that. The University of North Carolina will be happy to see me back."

Maria came in after Peter left, wearing a scowl on her face. "I don't know what's going on, but I don't like it. He should be in jail."

John turned to her and said, "Under normal circumstances you'd be right. But sometimes justice takes place outside the letter of the law. This was one of them, and if you're going to be in law enforcement long, you'll see it again." He looked away. "Besides, we really didn't have a solid case against him."

CHAPTER TWENTY-FOUR

It was a rare occasion when Riverview's annual July 4th family picnic, carnival, and rodeo wasn't blazing hot, but this year the Lord had mercy and not only sent low clouds but added a gentle breeze. This suited CJ down to her short socks and cross-trainer shoes. She admired her husband in his summer casual look of shorts, sandals, and a shirt depicting classic cars in bold primary colors.

They made their way toward the massive pecan and oak trees lining the river that formed the southern boundary of the park. David and Billy Paul came early that morning and made claim to a spot with thick grass and plenty of shade. Blankets and lawn chairs set the borders of the town's version of wooden stakes used to claim land in frontier days. It was a town tradition to get there no earlier than first light. Violators would have their blankets and lawn chairs placed in an area with sparse ground cover and no shade. The ladies from the senior adult classes of the town's churches strictly enforced the tradition and public shaming had always worked.

The bag CJ carried contained six dozen individually

wrapped snicker-doodle cookies, while David schlepped a cooler in each hand. The cookies were another part of the town's tradition. Strangers and town-folk alike were expected to take a walking tour by the river and sample cookies. This opened opportunities for conversations and sparked more than its fair share of romances.

Billy Paul and Aunt Bea were waiting with their basket of cookies, already open for business. Billy Paul issued his usual greeting of "Howdy," while Bea rose and passed out hugs. "Where's Nancy and little Davey?"

"They're coming," said CJ. "Had to stop and put some gas in her car. She thinks the E on the gas gauge means enough."

"Come sit by me. How are you feeling?"

"No problems. The doctor says I'm right on schedule but warned me about weight gain and eating salty foods."

Bea patted her hand. "They tell everyone that. Calories don't count on the Fourth of July. Are you staying for the fireworks?"

She looked at David, but he was already talking to Billy Paul. "We might. It depends on how tired I get. I slept in today, so there's a good chance we will."

"I've been meaning to ask you," said Bea. "I haven't heard anything about moonshine or that nasty fentanyl lately. Are they gone for good?"

"I don't know for how long, but things definitely changed when they made the big arrests in Killeen and a certain young man moved back to North Carolina."

"That's music to my ears. Our students have enough to keep them worried without that."

A young couple walking hand in hand stopped, and each took a cookie. Bea was on her feet. CJ was sure Bea had never met a person she didn't want to get to know.

After introducing herself and exchanging a few pleasantries, CJ lowered herself into a lawn chair and propped her feet up on a cooler. She'd be on her feet much of the day and didn't want to go home with ankles looking like stuffed sausages. Her chair was beside Billy Paul so she got in on the second half of a conversation.

"Does he still call you?" asked David.

"Every Wednesday night. I can set my watch by it. Asks the same questions and I give him the same answer." Billy Paul put his hand up to his face with his pinkie finger and thumb extended to mimic a telephone. "Yes, Pancho. Tig Murphy is still going to trial... Yes, Pancho. He'll go to prison. They have plenty of evidence against him... Yes, Pancho. He's the one responsible for the drug that killed your niece."

After pretending to hang up the make-believe phone, Billy Paul resettled his ball cap on his head. "I won't tell you what else he says, but I'm praying the case against Murphy is as solid as you say."

"I'm not involved anymore," said David. "But from what I'm hearing, they collected a van load of evidence from his house when they raided it. I don't see how he can beat the charges."

CJ interrupted. "Are you two going to talk shop all day? I heard a rumor they're serving fried peanut butter and jelly sandwiches at the carnival. I thought I might try one, or at least half of one. Anyone want to join me?"

"That might not be too bad," said Billy Paul. "Are they deep fried or fried in a skillet with butter on the bread?"

"Who cares?"

"Bring me back half."

David stood. "You'll be lucky to get it. If I'd known she was going to have such a craving, I would've bought stock in peanut butter."

She and David walked toward the sound of calliope music and followed the aromas of kettle corn, barbecue, and all things fried. Strange machines rose from the pasture. They tilted, spun, dipped, and rose again into the sky as screams of fear and delight mixed and mingled with the general noise of the crowd. Everyone entering the carnival area was forced to run the gauntlet of booths selling trinkets, gadgets, and toys that might or might not last until the end of the day. The next temptation was games of skill that involved rings and bottles, balloons and dull darts, baseball throws at fur-edged dolls and miniature rifles shooting cork bullets.

CJ challenged David to ring the bell on the pole by hitting a wooden block with an oversize mallet. He declined. While they watched from a distance, she noticed Randy come forward to take his turn after forking over a string of tickets. The weight sped upward, but stopped at number 95, only five shy of winning something. She hadn't noticed the girl until he returned to her side with a shrug of his shoulders that communicated, "Oh, well. I tried."

"Come on, David. Let's talk to Randy. I want to know how he's doing."

They intercepted the couple as they walked toward the Ferris wheel.

"Oh. Hi, Miss CJ." He looked a little apprehensive as he stuck out a hand. "Mr. David."

The two exchanged a shake that seemed to make Randy more at ease, but still nervous enough to not introduce the girl with him. About the same age as Randy, she wore pink shorts, a cotton blouse layered over a T-shirt and flat canvas shoes. They were approximately the same height but made a striking pair with his coal-black hair and her mane of long, blond tresses. She partially hid a pretty face behind glasses with pink frames.

CJ took over so as not to embarrass the girl for Randy's oversight. "I'm CJ Harper and this is my husband, David."

The girl's smile came across as genuine and confident. "I'm Lilly. Randy talks about you two all the time. He told me how much you helped him when he was in trouble." Her eyebrows raised. "Have you heard the good news?"

"Tell us," said David.

"His lawyer worked a miracle. No federal charges, and he only has to stay on probation for one year. We found out yesterday. That's why we're here celebrating."

"That's great," said CJ, pretending she didn't already know. "You'll have to come down to our picnic site and have some cookies and something cold to drink. Billy Paul and Bea are there."

Lilly's blue eyes sparked behind her glasses. "Billy Paul arranged for Randy to get hired at the Dodge dealership where I work in the title department with my mom. That's how we met." She smiled at Randy. "He's already received a pay raise."

Randy found his voice. "Better money than I expected, and the job comes with benefits."

"What does your mom think of you two dating?" asked David.

Lilly came forth with a cute laugh. "She wasn't crazy about us seeing each other at first, but Randy's growing on her."

CJ nodded her approval. She was about to suggest she and David search out the fried peanut butter and jelly sandwich when Randy asked, "Did you hear about the trailer and my dad's land?"

"I heard there was a tax lien on it," said David.

"Not now. The sheriff auctioned it on the courthouse steps. Best thing that ever happened to me. I found a nice efficiency apartment close to work."

The conversation reached that point where everyone had said enough. Handshakes and hugs made it official, and the two couples went their own ways. CJ slid her arm under David's. "How about that?"

The bill of his baseball cap came down and went back up.

"What was it John said when we scared Peter Starks back to North Carolina? It was something like 'justice sometimes takes place outside of the letter of the law.' I guess Randy is a good example of that."

"It's called mercy," said CJ. "Now have some on me and find the fried PB&J. I'm starving."

BY THE TIME they returned to the picnic area, little Davey was sitting at Billy Paul's feet, eating a cookie, and Nancy was nowhere to be seen. CJ settled into her chair. "I see a child, but no mother."

Bea waved away the comment. "She and two of her buddies are off riding that contraption that flips and turns ever' which way. They'd have a mess if I was to ride it."

"Don't even mention making a mess. I'm finally through with morning sickness and I hope that's one thing I never experience again."

A wide smile crossed Bea's face. "Here comes the most handsome couple in town."

CJ didn't have to turn to know Bob and Alice were on their way.

"Mind if we join the party?" asked David's father.

Alice dropped to her knees on the blanket and talked to little Davey in a mostly one-sided conversation. She pretended to take a nibble from a soggy cookie.

"We were about to give up on you," said David.

"Wedding plans, house plans, honeymoon plans, plans for Alice's new job, a plan to find her successor at ACU—you name it, there's a plan involved."

David asked, "What's your plan for picking out furniture?"

Bob looked at Alice and then back to David. "To make sure Alice has her credit cards while I work on a car."

"Wise man," said Billy Paul.

CJ joined Alice on the blanket. "How many more regents meetings will you have to attend?"

"Two. Possibly three if they drag their feet in finding a replacement."

David dredged an ice chest and came out with a bottle of water. "I thought they were in a hurry to get rid of you."

CJ gave the same look her mother gave her father when he said something she didn't approve of. "That's not a very diplomatic way of expressing yourself. Besides, it doesn't matter anymore."

Billy Paul broke in. "True, but you'd have been proud to see Alice handle that mini-rebellion."

Bob spoke up. "I'd like to at least hear about it. We were both single for so long, we have to be reminded we need to use words to communicate."

Alice opened her mouth to contradict him, but stopped. "I thought I told you."

"CliffsNotes, dear, are not the same as reading the book." He turned to Billy Paul. "Get her started. All she needs is a little encouragement."

People may have been milling all around, but the world shrank to only those in the tight circle of friends and family. "The meeting started right on time," said Billy Paul. "Right on time, one month late. After the usual boring stuff, we moved to new business. This was the first trap they tried to set for her."

"I'm not sure I'd call it a trap," said Alice.

"Sounded like one to me," countered Billy Paul. "They asked about moonshine on campus and what you'd done to get rid of it. That's when you pulled out John's report. It acknowledged there were some isolated instances of moonshine found on campus, but the number of reports were no higher than those of last spring's number of beer and hard liquor. Then they all but accused you of covering up a student operating a still and supplying moonshine to campus."

Alice didn't deny the account. "They were rather forceful."

"You sure shut 'em up quick when you told them a still had been in operation outside the city limits, but a current ACU student did not operate it. Also, John had in the report, that no alcohol from that still ever made it to campus."

"Tell them how Alice handled the moral turpitude charges," said Bob.

Alice looked up with a sly smile parting her lips. "That was rather fun."

"She let 'em walk all the way into the trap before she sprung it on 'em," said Billy Paul. "They presented a written report of every time she came to Bob's house, how long she stayed, and when they went anywhere together."

"That means they hired a private investigator," said David.

Billy Paul nodded. "Yep. Alice is calm and waits until the ringleader asked for her resignation."

"What happened then?" asked CJ.

Billy Paul took his time. He reached in a cooler and retrieved a Big Red soda. As he closed the lid, he continued. "Alice stands up, and without a word goes to the door where Bob's waiting for her."

Bob interrupted. "I want to tell this part. We walk in arm-in-arm and Alice says, 'I'd like to introduce you to my husband. We married over spring break. Since your report of my activities didn't start until after the break, I'd like to know how you can accuse me of violating any moral clauses in my contract. I'm sure you ladies and gentlemen would like to know him better, so I've asked my husband to come and give a brief history of his life.'"

It was Billy Paul's turn to interrupt. "The ones that were so dead-set on giving Alice a pink slip looked like they were sucking on a lemon."

Bob's wide smile showed he enjoyed telling the tale. "I took my time and gave them my history from diapers all the way until the State of Texas sent me a check for false imprisonment and Alice and I started courting. It was odd. No one mentioned moral turpitude when I was in the room. When I was done, Alice saw me to the door then went back to face the lions."

After a long drink of soda, Billy Paul resumed his narrative. "Everything was real quiet when Alice came back in and sat down. She gave every regent a good, long look. Then she said—"

Alice spoke in her leader's voice. "I appreciate that you are serious about protecting the integrity of this university, but some of you have assumed the worst of me and my husband. I hope you use this as a lesson to not formulate plans to destroy others' lives and reputations."

"You should have seen their jaws drop," said Billy Paul. "The main ones that set out to destroy her lost all credibility."

Alice raised her bottle of water in a form of toast. "All I can say is God protected me and I'm glad it's over."

Everyone raised a glass or bottle in a salute.

Halfway through the tale little Davey crawled up in Bea's lap and fell fast asleep holding a half-eaten cookie. She settled him on the blanket, stood and straightened her back. "Come on, Billy Paul. Let's take a stroll and see what cookies we can find."

Billy Paul was on his feet. "I could sure use something to munch on. CJ didn't bring me half of her fried sandwich."

"Sorry. It was so good I ate all of it."

David, CJ, Bob, and Alice stayed, passed out cookies, and

visited until the fireworks started. Once completely dark, the sky erupted in a display that exceeded expectations. When the last chords of accompaniment music and the thunderous booms faded, the group gathered the remnants of a fun-filled day and made their way to the parking lot.

On the way home, CJ mulled over the myriad of good things she'd seen and heard that day. Randy was landing on his feet financially, emotionally and romantically. The campus was relatively free of illegal drugs and alcohol, and Alice had outwitted some petulant regents once again. The judge set a late August date for Tig Murphy's trial, and David made no mention of a postponement.

She ran her hand over her stomach. The biggest blessing of all was the life growing inside of her. She concluded everything seemed perfect—until the truck jolted as two wheels dipped in a pothole. Was there such a thing as life going too smoothly?

CHAPTER TWENTY-FIVE

It was only ten-thirty in the morning, but beads of sweat rolled down CJ's back. The summer had been abnormally pleasant until the calendar flipped to August. The weather reporter could have taped the forecast on July thirty-first and rebroadcast it for the last three weeks. CJ decided as she walked back to her office that tomorrow she'd order iced coffee at the Campus Grind instead of hot.

A car wheeled into a parking spot as she approached the building and a woman jumped out with a cell phone in hand. She had highlighted blond hair cut in a wedge with the tips coming forward, trying to meet under her chin.

"Excuse me," she said. "Is this the campus police department?"

"It is until construction is complete on the new building. Can I help you?"

The woman came closer. She looked about the same age as many of the students on campus, but carried herself with more confidence. "I'm looking for the assistant chief of police. I believe her name is Catherine Jo Harper."

"You're in luck. I'm CJ Harper and I'm sweating. Let's go inside."

They stepped into the lobby as a student stood at the dispatcher's window, most likely paying a parking ticket. "Come back to my office and we can talk in private."

The woman introduced herself by stating her full name, but all CJ caught was the first name, Kiley. She was one of those women whose words spill out at an amazing rate of speed. What CJ heard clearly was the purpose of the woman's visit. "I'm a reporter for the Temple Telegraph. I wanted to give you an opportunity to respond to accusations that will appear in tomorrow's paper."

It might have been the baby choosing that moment to perform gymnastics inside her, but CJ knew it was more likely her stomach lurching. Instead of responding, she simply stared at the woman, too stunned to speak.

"As I'm sure you're well aware, the trial of Tiger Murphy begins next week. I've been told that part of his defense is to show you and your husband manufactured and planted evidence to incriminate Mr. Murphy."

CJ knew she had to be careful. "Told by whom?"

"What?"

"Who told you we manufactured and planted evidence?"

"I'm sorry, but my sources are strictly confidential."

CJ nodded she understood the non-answer by the reporter, as her stomach did another slow roll.

"It's public knowledge that you killed Mr. Murphy's brother when he allegedly attacked you. That led to your selection as a Texas Ranger, which you mysteriously turned down. My sources also tell me you refused the appointment because the incident wouldn't stand up under additional scrutiny."

CJ considered showing the pushy young reporter the scar on her face to prove an attack by a drug-addled psychopath, but sat with hands folded in front of her and mouth closed instead.

The reporter leaned forward and changed the tone of her voice to something less confrontational. "Look. This is your chance to deny the allegations against you and your husband. I'm trying to be fair as a journalist. Do you deny holding any animosity against Mr. Murphy?"

With everything in her, CJ wanted to shout her and David's innocence. She also wanted to grab the woman by her highlighted hair and throw her out of the building. Instead, she took a deep breath, let it out slowly and stood. She extended a hand toward the door. "University policy prohibits me from commenting on pending criminal cases. Contact the university's office of public affairs for official comments. I'm sure you can find your way out."

The shaking of her hands started as soon as the reporter turned her back. Her first inclination was to call David, but that proved to be an effort in futility. The call went directly to his voice mail.

She thought about going to John's office, shutting the door, screaming, and then telling him what happened. That wouldn't work, either. He'd taken the day off to take his family swimming.

What about Alice? She picked up her phone and called Alice's personal assistant.

"Sorry, Mrs. Harper. The other Mrs. Harper is with her Mr. Harper in the chapel, making final arrangements for their formal wedding ceremony." She paused. "That sounded odd, didn't it?"

"We're not a typical family."

On her way past the dispatcher, CJ hollered. "I'm going to the chapel. Call if you need anything."

"Did you catch Maria's radio traffic?"

"I just turned it on. What did she get into this time?"

"She stopped the Barbie Doll that left your office. Speeding and running a stop sign."

The door shut behind CJ before she smiled and whispered, "Who says there's no justice?"

With her mind still focused on the accusatory questions and the impending newspaper story, CJ decided to walk to the chapel. By the time she arrived, she was sweating for two. The weight she'd gained and the changes in body chemistry combined to make walking in August's heat almost unbearable. In acquiescence to her new norm, a treadmill and an extra-large fan sat in her bedroom. No more two-mile runs in the evening.

Despite the sweat rolling down her back, CJ breathed in and let go of the tension gripping her. The chapel was, beyond any doubt, her favorite building on campus. Local stones, hand hewn well over a century ago, formed the outside walls. The diffused light of stained glass windows running down each side of the sanctuary made the craftsmanship of the woodwork look flawless. She considered how special this place was, is, and would continue to be. This was the place she and David finally found peace when they lost their first child.

She expected to experience the same sense of peace when she pulled the heavy wooden door open, but that's not what she found. CJ recognized the two professors, one the head of the music department, and the other a producer of the university's theatrical productions.

The thespian spoke in a commanding voice. "I'm telling you, George, the music has to match the mood. It needs to be lively and joyous, not a funeral dirge."

The head of the music department lifted his chin to the point he looked down his nose at the shorter man. "And I say a woman of Alice's stature and grace needs music that matches her and the solemnity of the occasion. This isn't a barn dance, Stanley."

Alice sat with an arm draped over a pew, allowing the two to go at it. Bob sat far away from the fray. He looked up and nodded a greeting to CJ. Then he rose and tiptoed her way, motioning for her to sit on the back row.

She whispered before she sat down. "Do I need to send over a few officers in riot gear?"

Bob brushed away the suggestion. "This is nothing. You should have been here when the floral designer and the woman making Alice's dress got into it. I didn't know flowers had joy or apprehension and dresses captured the hopes and dreams of the bride." He looked at Alice and sighed. "If this keeps up, I'm going to suggest we elope again."

Bob turned his face to her. "What brings you out of an air-conditioned office today?"

"I need to talk to Alice. I had a reporter ambush me this morning. There's going to be a newspaper story that accuses me and David of some pretty nasty things."

"Like what?"

"Manufacturing and planting evidence. It all goes back to the biker I shot."

"Nonsense."

"Yes, we know that, but the public is pretty gullible."

Bob leaned in to her. "There was a former attorney that would come to the library where they had me working. He and I got to be pretty good friends." He paused. "Not good friends, but at least someone I could talk to on the same level. He wanted to know about mechanical engineering and I wanted to learn about law. Anyway, he told me that in high-profile cases, a talented lawyer will try the case in the press, before the real trial starts."

The more she thought about it, the more nonsensical her

fears sounded, but a lingering doubt wouldn't go away. "But what if the story is a total lie?"

Bob shrugged his shoulders. "That didn't matter. He didn't plan on using it in court. The thing is, it's impossible to un-hear something, especially if it comes from a source that claims to be neutral and people perceive to be halfway reliable."

The explanation made perfect sense from the viewpoint of legal strategy, but not from a moral point of view. "It's not fair or right." CJ crossed her arms.

"I didn't say it was. Neither did the disbarred attorney in prison with me."

"Sorry. I didn't mean to—"

A wave of his hand cut her off. "You didn't offend me. I find it refreshing that after all you've been through, you still have a strong sense of fair play. The world would be a better place if more people thought like you do."

"Thanks for the talk. I guess all I needed was a willing ear to listen to me. Tell Alice I stopped by, and nothing's wrong."

"Any time, and don't worry about a silly newspaper article. I've had plenty written about me and I'm still around."

She was halfway back to the office when her cell phone rang.

"Did you call?"

"Yeah, but I talked to your dad. He pulled me off the ledge."

"He's pretty good at that. What was the problem?"

"Newspaper reporter."

"A fast-talking gal with highlights?"

"That's her."

"I meant to warn you. Sorry. She came to see me yesterday. How did you handle her?"

CJ stopped. "Back up the truck. She came to see you

yesterday, and you didn't let me know she'd probably ambush me this morning?"

"It was nothing. I told her no comment before she could ask a question. You've dealt with the press long enough to recognize them and know they'll do anything for a story. No reason for you to get upset."

"Assume nothing about me while my hormones are jumping around like they're on pogo-sticks."

"Please tell me you didn't hurt her."

"She's going back to Temple with all the hair still on her head."

"That's a relief."

"She's not happy, though. Maria sent her home with a ticket for speeding and running a stop sign."

David's laugh put an end to a stressful morning. Almost. "What other tricks does Tig's attorney have up his sleeve?"

"We'll have to wait to find out. It's still odd they haven't asked for a postponement. Maybe they're waiting till the last minute. Captain Crow thinks they might even wait until jury selection starts."

"What do you think?"

"I think Tig's spending a lot of money on attorneys and he expects them to pull off a miracle."

CHAPTER TWENTY-SIX

Water ran in the bathroom sink as David collected everything needed to shave. CJ leaned her backside against the marble top on her side of the vanity and watched as he squirted shaving cream on his left hand and smeared the white foam from cheeks to throat. She loved to watch the contortions he made with his face early in the morning. She also took pleasure in seeing him with only a towel tucked around his waist.

He glanced over at her. "Are you ready for today?"

She looked down at her robe and house shoes. "It might be best if I show up wearing something a little more appropriate for a trial."

He made the first pass of the razor down his cheek and washed off the lather under running water. "The judge hearing the trial runs a tight ship. I doubt he'd let you in dressed like that." He puffed out a cheek and drug the razor down again.

"I thought you said you didn't expect the trial to start until late fall or even after the first of the year."

"I didn't," said David. "I was wrong. The defense never asked for a postponement."

She gave voice to a question she didn't expect an answer to. "I wonder why not?"

The grunt he made communicated he didn't know.

"Is the case really as air tight as you say it is?"

He stopped looking at his face in the mirror and turned his head. "From everything Blake told me, it's rock solid. The DNA from the trunk of the car matched Tig's, and the blood belonged to Amy. That gave the Bell County detectives what they needed to get a search warrant for Tig's house. That's where they hit the jackpot. They recovered the murder weapon and plenty of evidence related to his being the kingpin behind the drugs."

David went back to making funny faces as he worked around his mouth and under his nose. CJ voiced another concern. "I hope they don't ask me about the night I shot Tig's brother."

"That newspaper story was a flash in the pan. The editor made sure the reporter stuck to the facts. In the end, I think it did Tig more harm than good."

As the shaving exhibition continued, CJ pondered what the day might bring. People would likely fill the gallery to overflowing. Press would be there, including all the local outlets and perhaps some from Fort Hood. The trial would start with each attorney making opening statements.

"Honey," she said. "It didn't take long to complete *voir dire.*"

Once again, he stopped shaving and shook his razor at her. "That has me scratching my head, too. Captain Crow told me the district attorney couldn't explain it to him. He expected a lot of peremptory challenges to those selected to be jurors, but it was like both sides were looking for jurors with the same personalities."

"Personalities?"

The razor in David's hand became an extension of his fingers as he waved it around. "People who think in terms of black and white, right and wrong. Most defense attorneys look for compassionate people. Their second choice is those who are open to considering the facts from various points of view."

"I thought you said the defense team was some of the best in the area."

"Supposed to be."

He drew the razor down his neck, then back up, leaving only a little residual lather to rinse off.

"What's for breakfast?" she asked.

He grabbed a face towel and worked his way around the now-smooth face. "I thought we'd stop on the way. The trial doesn't start until ten and you're not scheduled to testify until after opening statements."

She hooked her fingers under the top of his towel and gave it a hard enough tug so it fell to the floor as she turned to find something to wear that fit over her baby bump. "Get dressed. I'm starving."

<hr>

DAVID HAD NOT SPOKEN since they left the courthouse in Belton. CJ let another mile pass before she interrupted his absent-minded tapping on the steering wheel. After they merged into traffic on southbound I-35, the silence got the better of her.

"How did my testimony go?"

He made no move to look at her. "Huh?"

"I asked what you thought of my testimony."

"It was fine."

Another mile of silence. More tattoos on the steering wheel.

"Did you notice Pancho Grimes?"

"Uh-huh."

David faced straight ahead, but his mind seemed to be back in the courtroom. She tried again. "The prosecuting attorney made it easy on us and the detectives from Bell County. The way he phrased his questions made it so all we had to do was answer yes or no."

"Uh-huh."

The memory of the testimony brought a smile to her lips. "I wish all district attorneys made it that easy on their witnesses. It made my time on the stand fly by."

"Mmm."

She reached over and patted his arm. "And then you took the stand and did the same thing."

She looked to her left, saw his creased brow and turned her head to look out her window at a patch of scorched grass, probably caused by a grass fire. Another mile passed.

"What's wrong, honey?"

The thumping of his finger stopped. "It was too easy."

"What was?"

"The defense passed on cross-examining you entirely. The only halfway serious question they had for me was if I had knowledge of a relationship between Muscles and Tig. Even after I said I didn't, they didn't hammer home the point."

"Why didn't they ask you about the lollipops you took to the lab in Austin? Don't they always challenge us about some procedure we might have missed?" Another mile passed with nothing but the wind to listen to. Finally, CJ spoke while looking out the window. "I bet the defense won't be as easy on the detectives from Belton tomorrow."

The observation didn't require an answer from David, so he didn't give one. He'd gone back to that place he sometimes went to mentally when things didn't add up. She decided he could worry for both of them if he wanted to, but she was moving on with life.

"David."

"Uh-huh."

"Alice and your dad are getting back from their honeymoon tonight."

"Mmm."

"She called me today. She's pregnant, too."

David's head jerked to the right and so did the SUV. His mouth opened, but nothing came out.

It was the best laugh she'd had in a month of Sundays. One of those that went on and on. David had been in some tight spots in the army and law enforcement, but she'd never heard anyone say he showed fear. The look on his face when he thought he was going to be a father and a half-brother all at the same time was one of sheer panic.

After he ranted for three miles, she defended herself. "It serves you right for worrying so much and not talking to me. Nothing will go wrong. You'll see."

She didn't know if she believed the words, but it pulled David out of his shell. He'd forgotten about his dad and Alice getting back from Rome. It also must have slipped his mind that Alice was well past child-bearing age.

CHAPTER TWENTY-SEVEN

People were still filing into the courtroom when David snagged two seats beside Billy Paul. "I didn't expect to see you here."

"Got a phone call last night. Pancho Grimes wanted me to come. Said he didn't understand what was going on yesterday."

"I saw him, but didn't speak to him. CJ did and you're right, all the legal talk made little sense to him."

Billy Paul scanned the courtroom. "Where's CJ?"

"Freshening up."

Their neighbor's blue eyes seemed to smile. "I hear a baby in the oven has a way of making women freshen up often."

"Amen to that."

At that moment CJ and Pancho walked in, one after the other, and sat where David pointed. He thought it might be advisable to put Pancho between them, just in case Pancho had a spell of inappropriate behavior. Today, his dress was the same as yesterday. In fact, he thought they were the same clothes: long sleeve denim work shirt with snap buttons, blue jeans, black belt, scuffed brown work boots, and a baseball cap emblazoned with decals and pins showing he'd served in Afghanistan.

Billy Paul gently reminded Pancho to remove his cap. There was a lag between the time the message reached Pancho and he complied. It didn't seem to be an act of rebellion, only a delay in processing the meaning.

Pancho turned to Billy Paul. "Will this be over today? I hope so. I'm tired of driving all the way from deep East Texas."

David fielded the question for Billy Paul. "It may go on a week or more. He's charged with a lot of crimes and there's a lot of people who have to testify against him."

"Then he'll go to prison for killing Holly. Right?"

Billy Paul took the heat off of David. "That's what the lawyer on the right side is trying to do. The one on the left is trying to keep him out of prison."

Pancho's head wagged. "Why would he do that if everyone knows he's a bad man?"

"That's the way the law works," said Billy Paul.

"Ain't right."

The bailiff stood. In a booming voice he commanded, "All rise!"

The second day of the trial started right where the first left off. The judge reminded everyone about courtroom decorum and that he wouldn't tolerate outbursts. As expected, the two deputies from Bell County testified, the younger following the elder. The prosecution followed the same pattern of asking questions in a way that produced simplified answers and laid the groundwork for what was to come. The seizing, transport, and turning over of the car to a police impound yard with constant surveillance went without the defense objecting. The detectives also testified they followed the car from the used car lot, observed the tow driver loading and unloading it, and kept it in sight all the way until forensic experts took over.

With Pancho leaning forward, CJ caught David's attention and whispered, "That's four witnesses in a row that those high-priced lawyers haven't tried to discredit anything. I'm getting worried."

He thought about saying something to reassure her, but an invisible imp had already whispered doubt in his ear. He mentally shook it off and said, "Everything's fine so far."

The next witnesses to testify were the duo that made up a forensic team. They explained their job was to gather evidence from crime scenes. The first went into excruciating detail on how he had gathered samples of carpet, of suspicious stains on the seats, and of contents of the interior of the car, and even used a vacuum on every nook and cranny inside the car. The interior and exterior of the car was also dusted for fingerprints, resulting in the lifting of many prints.

The DA asked, "After you gathered this evidence, what did you do?"

"I placed the individual pieces of evidence in plastic evidence bags, and I identified each one as to its place of origin in the car. I wrote the date, time, and my name on the chain of custody tag. This included the small bag from the vacuum."

"Was the vacuum clean before you used it?"

"It's always cleaned after each use and double checked before it's used again."

"Did you make sure the vacuum was clean before using it on this occasion?"

"Yes, and I never reuse a bag."

"Is it true you did not process any of the material found inside the trunk of the car?"

"That's correct."

"Is it true that Bell County contracts with an accredited forensic laboratory to conduct testing on evidence gathered?"

"Yes, except for fingerprint identification. That's handled in-house by submitting them to several national and state agencies."

It was the defense's turn, and David leaned forward, intent on hearing every word.

"No questions for the witness," said one of the three attorneys at the table. "With the court's permission, we would like to reserve the right to cross-examine at a later time, if additional testimony conflicts with what the witness has presented or clarification is needed."

"Granted," said the judge. He looked at his watch. "There's time for one more before we break for lunch. Bailiff, call the next witness."

A woman who'd been waiting in the hallway made her way down the center aisle where the bailiff met her, swung open a spring-hinged gate, and allowed her access to the area that separated the gallery from the almost mythical area on the other side of 'the bar.' He directed her to the witness stand, where he swore her in and invited her to be seated.

CJ whispered. "She doesn't look a day over eighteen. The defense may eat her for lunch."

"She's a pretty little thing," said Pancho out loud. "Reminds me of Holly."

Billy Paul and David both turned to Pancho as several nearby people snickered.

The judge's gavel came down. "Quiet! I'll not give another warning."

Billy Paul whispered for Pancho to be quiet. David issued a hard stare to let Pancho know he'd breached etiquette.

The prosecuting attorney began with a repeat of his prior questioning. He established education and training credentials for the woman who gathered forensic evidence from the car.

"She's older than I thought," whispered CJ. "And smarter."

David grunted and wiped his hands on his trousers. Would the woman be able to hold her own? She soon had her opportunity.

"Ms. Stockridge," said the prosecuting attorney. "What made you think the stain in the trunk was blood?"

"I wasn't sure until I cut a small section out of the carpet, took it to a dark room, sprayed it with luminal, and looked at it under a black light."

An attorney from the defense table stood. "Your Honor, we move this testimony be stricken from the record and the jury instructed to ignore it. The prosecution did not present the entire carpet from the trunk in discovery and this small sample is therefore inadmissible."

The prosecuting attorney took a step forward. "Your Honor. The entire section of carpet wasn't needed. The sample piece was available to the defense and they conducted their own test. The test Ms. Stockridge referred to showed the victim's blood on it and is a linchpin to this case."

The judge looked at the defense counsel over his glasses. "Are you disputing the results of the testing?"

"No, Your Honor."

"Objection overruled."

"Score one for the prosecution," said CJ in hushed words.

The prosecuting attorney went right to his next question. "In your testimony, you said you noticed a single hair lying on the carpet in what you thought might be blood. Is that right?"

"That's correct."

"And you also testified you were fully gowned in a hazmat suit with a face shield and rubber gloves on. Is that correct?"

"And booties made from the same material as the coveralls," she replied.

"Tell me how you were able to see a single hair in a dark trunk?"

"The trunk wasn't dark. We used shop lights and I never leave home without my flashlight in my pocket." She reached in her coat pocket, produced a small cylinder, and pushed a button on the back of it. She shined it in the attorney's eyes, which caused him to turn his head.

"Pretty bright, huh?"

The judge chuckled, composed himself, and asked, "Any more questions for this witness?"

"No, Your Honor."

"Counsel for the defense, do you wish to cross examine this witness?"

"No, Your Honor."

"We'll reconvene at one-thirty."

"NOT AS MANY people here this afternoon," said David as he looked at a smattering of empty seats.

CJ cast her gaze at the rows in front of her. "There's still ten minutes before court reconvenes. What did Captain Crow have to say when you called him?"

"It surprised him the defense hasn't done more to challenge witnesses."

Billy Paul and Pancho brushed past them, putting an end to talking as freely as they normally would. CJ leaned in front of David and caught Pancho's attention. "Tell me about your land in East Texas, Pancho. Do you raise any crops?"

"It's mainly woods that's been in my family for a long time. I plant a small garden, but I ain't much on growin' things. When I ain't diggin' holes for septic tanks, I hunt and fish."

"Did I hear you say that you live on the land and not in town?"

"Don't like town. My cabin is quiet."

CJ leaned back, putting an end to the brief conversation. David continued to scan the crowd and didn't have long to wait before the bailiff commanded everyone to stand.

The first witness of the afternoon identified himself as a forensic lab technician. Education and professional credentials came next, and the prosecuting attorney launched into his normal pattern of asking questions that required little of the witness other than to say yes or no.

Holding up a plastic bag, an assistant district attorney asked, "Do you recognize this evidence bag, and is this your signature on it?"

"Yes."

The attorney looked at the judge. "I'd like to enter this as Exhibit 4."

The judge asked, "Does the defense have an objection?"

"No objection."

Step by methodical step, the prosecution walked the accredited scientist through explaining that human blood stained the carpet, and that the DNA results proved a positive match to the blood found in the car's trunk and to that of Amy Sneller.

Next, the prosecution sought and received permission to enter evidence in a second bag. This one contained the single hair found in the blood.

"And did you run a DNA test on the hair?" asked the prosecuting attorney.

"Yes."

"Did you find a match?"

"The results showed a near one-hundred percent match to that of the defendant, Mr. Tig Murphy."

David let out a tense breath. They made the link between Tig Murphy and the murder of Amy Sneller.

The defense attorney rose. David noted this one had not spoken up to this point. His black and gray hair was slicked back and his dark suit looked tailored to fit his thin frame. He asked the judge's permission to examine the plastic bag of evidence containing the single hair. The judge granted his request.

He took the bag to where the witness sat in an elevated seat. "Mr. Crenshaw," said the attorney in a drawl that dripped with polite charm. "Did I hear you correctly when you said you took possession of all the samples of evidence gathered by the two people who testified before lunch?"

"That's correct."

"And that includes the one I'm holding now?" He moved closer and his hand held out the plastic bag for the witness to examine.

"Yes."

"And this is your name on the tag that records the chain of custody?"

"Yes. That's my name."

The attorney seemed to move in slow motion, like it was too warm to use much energy. He looked at the card again. "It certainly is your name on the card."

He stepped away, looked at the jury and turned back to the witness. "Before you answer this next question, Mr. Crenshaw, I want you to take your time. I also want to remind you of the oath you've taken to tell the truth. The penalty for violating that oath can, and likely will, have serious consequences."

The courtroom hushed to what seemed like absolute silence. A knot developed in David's stomach and he didn't believe it was from the enchiladas he had for lunch.

The defense attorney moved close to the witness. "I want

to tell you something you may not know, Mr. Crenshaw. I have two nationally known handwriting experts that will testify if you don't tell the truth."

He let the words sink in before he raised his voice in a loud, accusatory tone. "Is this your signature on the evidence tag?"

David knew the answer. The attorney wouldn't have asked if he didn't know the answer would benefit his client.

Mr. Crenshaw hesitated. His gaze shifted from side to side and then fell to a spot on the floor. His response came out as a weak and pitiful, "No."

An audible gasp came from those in the courtroom who knew what would happen next. Right on cue, the defense attorney turned to the judge and spoke loud enough for all to hear. "Your Honor, we move for a mistrial."

The prosecutor rose immediately from his chair. "Your Honor. This is but one piece of evidence we have to submit that will show conclusively—"

The defense attorney shouted over him. "The chain of custody is broken. This evidence pertaining to the admission of the single hair found in the car is tainted beyond redemption. Any subsequent search warrants or actions taken by police based on discredited evidence are inadmissible under the long-standing doctrine of fruit of the poisonous tree."

The judge's gavel fell. "Both counsels. In my chambers. Now!" He looked down at the witness. "Don't go anywhere, Mr. Crenshaw. You and I are going to have a talk."

CJ placed her elbows on her knees with her cheeks in the palms of her hands and moaned, "It's over."

"What's goin' on?" asked Pancho. "We just went to lunch. They can't be hungry."

Billy Paul put a calloused hand on Pancho's shoulder. "Things aren't looking good."

"Why not? He sold drugs that killed Holly. He also killed

that other college girl. They found his hair in her blood, didn't they?"

David didn't want to respond, and Billy Paul kept silent. CJ lifted her head and got Pancho's attention. "Someone didn't follow the rules. It's possible Tig Murphy won't go to prison."

David added, "At least not this time around."

The muscles in Pancho's cheeks flexed. He spoke through clenched teeth, loud enough to be heard, but it didn't seem like he was talking to anyone but his niece, Holly Grimes. "Don't worry, sugar. I'll take care of the man who killed you."

CJ and David traded a look of concern but said nothing.

The noise in the room continued to rise as long minutes passed. Some reporters had sprinted out of the courtroom at the first opportunity to where cameras waited in the hall. One by one they filtered back in, checked to make sure they missed nothing, and held their phones at the ready.

Hoping against hope, David waited. The attorneys filed in, each wearing a poker face that revealed nothing. The judge entered and gave the command for everyone to sit. Those present did, albeit on the edge of their seats.

"In the case of the State of Texas v Murphy, I have no recourse available to me but to declare a mistrial. The defendant is free to go."

"Just as well," said Pancho. "Now I get to do things my way."

David had seen the look in Pancho's eyes before. It came to soldiers after they'd lost a member of their squad. Revenge had a look all its own.

CHAPTER TWENTY-EIGHT

CJ fanned smoke away from the kitchen's smoke detector. No luck. The ear-piercing beeps went unabated even though she'd opened the back door and turned on the ceiling fan. A trivet sat under the skillet containing what should have been a part of their breakfast. She'd reduced the bacon to something no self-respecting ant would eat.

"Are you serving burnt offerings again?" asked Nancy as she entered with Davey on her hip.

CJ quit fanning long enough to say, "Not today, young lady. I'm in a bit of mood and you know what you can do if you don't like my cooking."

The chastisement didn't seem to faze her. "I'll pick up breakfast at the Campus Grind and they'll feed Davey at early childhood development."

Little Davey pinched his nose with chubby fingers and babbled an unknown word of displeasure.

Nancy looked at CJ. "Out of the mouths of babes..."

"Call if you're going to be late," said CJ as she shooed mother and son out the door.

The smoke alarm was still making its presence and functionality known when David came from the direction of his office. "I asked you to watch the stove. What happened?"

"Don't blame me. You're the one who ran out before I could say anything."

"I'm listening now. What were you doing that was so important you almost caught the kitchen on fire?"

"Well..."

"As I suspected. You weren't paying attention."

Her voice raised a couple of notches. "You're not the only one that receives important phone calls around here."

His raised eyebrows asked for a more complete explanation.

"It was Alice." CJ turned her back on David to see if the pan had cooled enough to throw away the evidence of her latest culinary disaster.

"Well? What did she want?"

"To talk."

David huffed. "About what?"

The smoke alarm mercifully ended its racket.

Speaking in a lower volume, CJ said, "This and that. Checking on the baby and how I'm doing. She gave me a report on when the concrete company will pour the slab for their home. She also said Randy found another car your dad might be interested in restoring."

After pouring himself a fresh cup of coffee, David turned again to face her. "Anything else?"

"Nothing much. Only that she won't be our state representative. And... the regents are begging her to stay."

The mug was halfway to David's lips when she broke the last two pieces of news, and there it stayed, suspended in space. He came to his senses. "Start with the part about her not being a state representative."

"I told you several weeks ago our state rep went to a

specialist at the Mayo Clinic. They found out what was really wrong with him, and he's well on his way to being back to his old self. He withdrew his resignation. That left Alice without a new job to go to."

"Did she just find out?"

CJ nodded. "As soon as he started feeling better, he asked the governor to postpone the announcement. He never officially resigned, so there's not much the governor could do but apologize to Alice."

"She'll continue on as president of ACU?"

"Your dad thinks it's a good idea, but he wants her to keep the regents guessing for a while longer. She's all for it since the ones that wanted her scalp have come around."

David looked at another skillet that would most likely need to be thrown away. "No wonder you burned the bacon."

Sandy came in through the doggy door, sniffed, looked at the skillet, and then at CJ. If a dog could speak, she'd be asking, "Again?"

CJ never claimed she could cook, but when your dog gives you a look of disappointment, it's time to go on the offensive. "What was so important about your phone call you couldn't cook breakfast?"

David must have been processing the multiple pieces of information, because it took him several seconds to respond. His gaze fixed on something out by the barn, and he answered the question in a monotone. "Blake called. In the very early hours this morning, Bell County deputies and state troopers responded to a call from Tig's home. One of the delivery drivers that was to testify against Tig is dead. That Russian guy we call Muscles hasn't been located, and Tig Murphy is nowhere to be found."

"Holy smoke! Was Tig tying up loose ends?"

"That's what I thought at first."

"What makes you say that?"

"Blake told me it looked like someone started cleaning the scene, but didn't get very far."

CJ went to the pantry, retrieved a box of cereal, and shuffled to the refrigerator for milk. On her way to get a bowl, she stopped. "Why does Blake think it might be someone else?"

"They found dirt on the floor that didn't match anything on Tig's shoes or boots. He's convinced Tig will show up in a day or two with an air-tight alibi."

The tone of his voice held enough skepticism to make her think David wasn't so sure Blake had it figured correctly. She moved everything she needed to the table for a quick breakfast. "Come join me and tell me why you think Blake's wrong."

He moved his mug from the granite countertop and pulled out a rolling chair. A long pause followed as David settled in the chair and took a drink of coffee. She knew he was stalling, looking for the right words.

"I can't help but remember what Pancho said and the look in his eyes at Tig's trial."

CJ dropped her spoon in her bowl, sending a few drops of milk flying. "That possibility hadn't crossed my mind. What are you going to do?"

He ran his finger around the rim of the mug. "My first inclination is to do nothing, at least for now. If Tig and Muscles don't show up in a few days, I'm not sure what I'll do."

"Have you told Blake or Captain Crow what Pancho said at the trial and how he acted?"

The only response was a shake of his head.

"You'd better do it soon."

"Why?"

"What do you mean, why?"

David stood, went to the door, and looked through one of the mullioned glass panes. "Let's say Pancho took matters into his own hands. The DA was going for life in prison. Staying locked in prison until you die isn't too different from what Pancho wanted to do to Tig. Some would say it's more humane to give someone like Tig a quick death as opposed to a slow one."

"Are you serious?" She'd never heard David speak like this. She pushed her bowl of cereal away and faced him. "I can't believe you could even think like that, let alone put words to it."

David shrugged and turned to her. "Sometimes I think too much. Talk is all it was. I'll call Blake in a little while and tell him what we saw and heard." He took another sip of coffee. "Blake's probably right. Tig and Muscles will show up in a day or two and we'll have to start all over."

David returned to his office and CJ pulled her bowl of cereal back to her and took a bite. As she chewed, she thought of the possibility that Pancho might have abducted Tig Murphy... or worse.

CHAPTER TWENTY-NINE

First light broke on what promised to be a hot mid-September day as David stopped for snacks on his way to Pancho's land in deep East Texas. He grabbed a couple packs of peanuts, an energy drink, and two bottles of water. Blake Cruz took his load of snacks and drinks to the counter and pulled out his debit card. The trip to Upshire County would take over three hours and was a journey they both dreaded. *Conflicted* was the word Blake used, and David couldn't agree more. If things panned out the way they expected, Pancho would be in handcuffs today.

Back on the road, they headed northeast out of Waco, on their way to Tyler, Gilmer, then somewhere off a dirt road this side of Ore City. David turned to Blake, who was polishing off the first of two jelly-filled pastries. "Are you positive Muscles' alibi checks out?"

Blake dragged a napkin across his lips before he answered. "He was at a casino in Oklahoma all day and night. No way he could have been at Tig's home."

David shook his head. That bit of information eliminated

Muscles and put the spotlight on Pancho. "How close was the match of the dirt found at Tig's home to Pancho's land?"

"Close," said Blake, as he licked glaze off his fingers. "It had a high concentration of iron, just like dirt from Ore City. That explains why it was so red. Not much of that around Central Texas. The dirt and the threats you reported Pancho made were enough to get a search warrant, but it won't be near enough to put Pancho away if we don't find a body or some other evidence."

David remained silent, but Blake didn't mind expressing his thoughts. "It would be a crying shame if we have to arrest Pancho. Things are quiet since Tig went missing. Not one case of fentanyl overdose since the trial. If Pancho put that good-for-nothing in the ground, I'm inclined to say he did the people of the state a favor."

Even though David agreed with Blake, he learned a long time ago that sometimes a nod, or a well-placed grunt, kept him out of trouble. He replied with both.

The miles clicked by, as did the small towns, until they reached Tyler, a good-sized city that slowed their progress. From Tyler they headed northeast to Gilmer, the county seat. The roads narrowed as they transitioned from farm to market roads, to paved county roads, to unpaved but maintained county roads, to a private red-dirt trail through the woods.

Pines stretched upward and locked arms overhead. From time to time, openings gave glimpses of a cloudless sky.

An Upshire County pickup truck was parked by a sturdy metal gate left open. Signs warning away trespassers deco-rated both the fence and gate. A deputy exited his truck and ambled to David's side of the SUV.

"You two the Rangers we're expecting?" His drawl was thick as cold molasses.

David motioned to Blake with an outstretched thumb. "Ranger Cruz, and I'm Sergeant Harper. Is everyone here?"

"All but the cadaver dog. They'll be here directly. The sheriff and a few others are at Pancho's cabin."

Pine needles covered the ground under the canopy of trees, while two red grooves made a straight path to a clearing and a small cabin. A trio of law enforcement vehicles parked along the trail, as did a pickup attached to a trailer topped with a backhoe.

Blake pointed to a backhoe close to the cabin and stated the obvious. "That must be what Pancho uses to dig holes for septic tanks. Not as big as I thought it would be."

David agreed. "Pancho has a reputation for being a slow worker. They limit him to digging holes for the smaller tanks."

"How far down would you say Pancho's backhoe can dig?"

David took a good, hard look. "I'd say about eight feet at the most. Maybe only six or seven."

Something else caught David's eye, a hand-painted sign nailed to the side of the cabin. It read: NOWHERE TEXAS. POPULATION 1.

The sheriff, a man with sharp facial features, greeted them and opened the conversation with words that seemed to match everyone's sentiments. "I don't mind telling you two, I'd be a happy man if we come up empty handed. Pancho Grimes was one of the finest young men this county ever produced. He still is. It's a shame what that IED did to him."

"I couldn't agree more," said Blake. "But the evidence is pointing to him and we have to see this through."

The sheriff turned his head at the sound of clattering coming their way. "There's the dog. This shouldn't take long, if there's something down there."

"You found the site?" asked David.

The sheriff's straw cowboy hat dipped as he nodded. "There's a clearing about a quarter mile from here. We served the warrant on Pancho at dawn, searched his cabin, and scouted the woods. He wouldn't tell us what he buried, but you'll see he put something in the ground and used his backhoe to do it."

A pickup truck with a dog kennel in the bed parked behind the truck and trailer carrying a backhoe larger than Pancho's.

"Let's get this over with," said the sheriff. He hollered at a deputy to bring Pancho out of his cabin, then climbed into his SUV and led the way. David parked in the shade as Blake opened his door and said, "Whatever happens, I hope it doesn't take long. It's already over ninety."

The vehicles parked in a semi-circle around a pile of red dirt in an oval-shaped clearing. The backhoe operator moved to the trailer and loosened chains that held his equipment in place. While that was going on, Blake went to speak to the man who brought the cadaver dog.

David joined the sheriff and took a position beside Pancho.

"That's a nice dog," said Pancho. "Is he one of those trained sniffer dogs like we had in the army?"

The sheriff confirmed Pancho's question, while David wondered how Pancho would react to seeing him again. He didn't have long to wait.

"You're that lawman that was at the trial with that tall, pretty lady. Is she your wife?"

"She is," said David, relieved that Pancho's voice carried no animosity.

"Don't you live close to Mr. Billy Paul?"

"We share a fence line."

Pancho's head nodded as he thrust his hands in the back pockets of dirty jeans. "He's a good man."

David agreed but didn't say so. By this time, Pancho had cast his gaze to the dog handler. The cadaver dog bounded down from the bed of the truck and strained at his leash. The handler played out slack and the dog made a bee-line to the mound of red dirt. With ears standing erect and tail waiving like the baton of a hyperactive band conductor, the mixed breed zig-zagged. It only took a few seconds before the dog sneezed and sat without moving.

The handler praised the dog, gave him a ball to play with, and walked to Blake. "There's something dead under that mound."

David's heart didn't sink all the way into his boots, but this wasn't the news he wanted to hear.

The tilt trailer carrying the backhoe slammed to the ground when the weight of the tractor passed the center of gravity. It wasn't long before the machine had its stabilizing outriggers extended and gouged buckets of iron-rich dirt out of the earth. David estimated the depth to be at about five feet when the bucket deposited something more than dirt.

The sheriff hollered and motioned for the driver to stop digging and cut off the tractor.

Lawmen, the dog, the handler, and Pancho gathered around what looked to be a section of ribs and what might be a piece of an arm. The handler leaned closer to the find and gave it a thorough visual inspection. He looked up at Pancho. "You must be a hunter."

Pancho grinned. "Hunting and fishing keeps me from going to the store so often."

The handler cast his gaze to the sheriff. "Deer. Nothing human so far."

"Killed it 'bout three weeks ago. Clean shot with a bow," said Pancho with pride in his voice.

"Let's keep going," said the sheriff. "There might be something else a little deeper."

After an hour of digging, the remains of the deer, including the lop-sided rack of an atypical buck, had long played out. David stared at a twelve-foot-deep hole in a clearing, surrounded by forest, in the middle of Nowhere, Texas. Pancho might get a ticket for shooting a deer out of season, but David didn't think so. Sometimes the law was best served by looking the other way.

Blake and David waited until they had the air conditioner on full blast before they called Captain Crow and gave him the report. He expressed his instructions to them in a way that left no room for misunderstanding.

"You two did right in following up on the evidence you had, but Pancho Grimes is off the list of suspects. The case will remain open, but I won't waste any more time or money on it. I don't know where Tig Murphy is, and I don't really care as long as he's not anywhere near Central Texas. You two stop by my office when you get back in town. I have new assignments waiting for you."

CHAPTER THIRTY

Gravel crunched under the tires of Nancy's car as she and Davey headed to town and another day of fall classes and child care at ACU. David and CJ both waved goodbye and walked to the carport. She slipped her hand over his bicep and gave it a not-too friendly squeeze.

"Why did you sidestep questions about yesterday's trip to East Texas?"

He looked down at the six-month baby bump and smiled. "What time is your doctor appointment?"

"Nine o'clock, and don't change the subject."

He stopped once they were under the covering of the carport. "I didn't want to go into the gory details of digging up deer remains in front of Nancy. Her curiosity would have led to a hundred questions I didn't want to answer this morning." David took a breath. "It's your fault for not staying awake until I got home. I would have told you, but these days you're sleeping for two."

She pulled his arm until he turned to face her. "Strap a fanny pack full of rocks to your stomach and see how tired you are. I'm not asleep now. Tell me what happened."

He huffed out a breath. "I drove almost four hours. The dog alerted to something dead and buried. The backhoe operator dug up the remains of a deer Pancho shot three weeks ago. We dug as deep as the backhoe could reach and found nothing else. Captain Crow, Blake, and the sheriff marked Pancho off the suspect list. I drove back to Waco. Captain Crow gave Blake and me new assignments. I drove home. End of story."

"Not so fast. I didn't hear your name among the people who took Pancho off the list."

David hooked his thumbs in his belt on either side of the buckle. "It doesn't matter what I think. We followed the evidence, executed a valid search warrant, and came up blank. I don't decide when to back off a case."

"So that's it?" asked CJ.

He nodded.

"I don't like it."

"Why not?"

She tented her hands on her hips. "Because you and I both know there's probably another hole in East Texas with Tig Murphy in it."

He put a hand on her shoulder. "Without additional proof, there'll never be another search warrant issued for Pancho's land."

CJ's eyebrows pulled together. "That doesn't bother you?"

David stepped away and looked at the sun rising. He lowered his voice. "It bothers me, but so do multiple deaths from fentanyl overdoses and cold-blooded murders." He formed a circle by touching the tip of his index finger to his thumb. "That's how many deaths by overdose and murders we've had since Tig went missing."

He considered reminding her she'd not hesitated to bend the truth and pressure Peter Starks into moving back to

North Carolina. It was another one of those times when it seemed best not to speak.

All he heard was a huff of disgust as her footfalls faded. Perhaps she was right and Captain Crow, Blake, and the sheriff were all wrong. Wasn't truth the goal of law enforcement? He concluded it to be too weighty a question to ponder long. He'd wrestle with the moral dilemma some other time. For now, he needed to give Billy Paul a report on Pancho.

DUMP TRUCKS LINED up six deep, waiting to get in Billy Paul's rock quarry as a steady stream of full trucks left. Crushed stone for road base and every other construction need imaginable had made Billy Paul a rich man. The line of trucks and rail cars waiting to be loaded insured he'd be richer by the end of the day. David parked outside an office building, well away from the worst of the noise generated by giant machines grinding big rocks into smaller ones and heavy machinery loading trucks and train cars, one after the other.

Billy Paul exited the building as David approached. "Howdy. What brings you out?"

"I wanted to give you a report on my trip to see Pancho Grimes."

Billy Paul pointed to an excavator parked at the far end of a large open space. "Funny you should mention Pancho. He helped me sell that used excavator. Took it to Tyler to show a company for me and brought it back while they decided. A semi pulling a low-boy trailer should be here any minute to pick it up."

Right on cue, a big-rig eased to a crawl. Billy Paul motioned the driver to pull to the far end of the lot where the machine sat.

"I remember you saying something about a new excavator," said David. "Who did you say bought this one?"

"The company's out of Tyler, but they do most of their work north of there."

The two walked toward the massive machine and talked as they went. "I wanted you to know we thought Pancho might've had something to do with Tig Murphy's disappearance. We dug up what looked like a fresh grave. All that was in it was hide and bones from a deer Pancho killed."

Billy Paul kept his gaze on the machine. "He told me he hunted and didn't much care what the law said about licenses or hunting seasons."

As they approached the machine, David inspected it with care. "That arm and bucket are over twice the size of the backhoe they used yesterday. How far down will it dig?"

"About twenty-five feet."

They moved to a spot where the bucket curled under the arm. David reached out and pulled off a chunk of rusty-red dirt from one of the bucket's teeth. He scrutinized it and looked at Billy Paul. Then, he threw it to the ground.

"I wanted you to know Pancho is no longer a suspect." He paused. "Even so, it might be a good idea if he stayed on his property unless he has legitimate business elsewhere. If you happen to talk to him again, tell him that."

"I doubt I'll be talking to him again. Some things are best left unsaid."

"The same thought occurred to me this morning."

Thanks for reading *A Grave Secret.* I hope it satisfied your appetite for a good whodunit. If it kept you turning the pages past your bedtime, then I've done my job! I'd be very grateful if you would take a minute to leave a review at your favorite retail site, Bookbub or Goodreads. Reviews are the lifeblood of books and you, the reader, can keep that lifeblood flowing!

To stay abreast of all my book news, join my Mystery Insiders community. As a thank you, I'll send you *Back Road Justice,* a David and CJ short story.

You can also follow me on Amazon, Bookbub and Goodreads to receive notification of my latest release.

Thanks again for reading!
Bruce

Scan above to sign up or go to bit.ly/Back-Road-Justice.